Fog Valley

by Joanna Metzger
Illustrated by Luke Mays

For Haley, Emilie, Tommy, Julia, Jacob, Elsa, Gavin and Levi—
all the little monsters in my life—J.M.

To my dad, Forrest Mays—L.M.

For information contact:
Mondo Publishing
980 Avenue of the Americas
New York, NY 10018
Visit our website at www.mondopub.com
Printed in USA
09 10 11 12 13   9 8 7 6 5 4 3 2 1
ISBN 978-1-60201-973-7

Design by Josh Simons, Simonsays Design!

Contents

ISAAC VON ULF

Chapter One

The Last Straw

Jason Crawford wasn't quite sure why this was the last straw. He didn't know which of his other actions had counted as straws, or how many other straws had led up to this final one. After spending a considerable amount of time analyzing it, he eventually decided that there really was no use wondering–anything was possible when it came to Agnes.

When Jason was just two years old, his mother decided she would leave the family to join a traveling circus. Her lifelong dream had been to become a lion trainer, and with a traveling circus in town, she saw her chance to turn fantasy into reality. Mr. Crawford had begged and pleaded with his wife to change her mind, but it was no use. Tired and helpless, he and little Jason watched as Mrs. Crawford packed a suitcase, climbed into a clown car, and rode into the sunset to pursue her dream.

After his wife left, Mr. Crawford found that his hands were full. Single-handedly he tried to take care of Jason and keep up the house, while still managing to report to his job at the chewing gum factory. But things became sticky very quickly.

One morning after having been awake for 48 hours straight, exhaustion finally set in as Jason's father packaged sticks of gum on the assembly line. As he slipped the last piece of Apple-Kiwi Gooey Chewy Bubblegum into its package, Mr. Crawford fell asleep. He swayed back and forth and landed facedown on the conveyor belt. If his shoulder hadn't brushed against a switch, no one would have noticed Mr. Crawford sleeping. But that did happen, causing the belt to go into reverse. The very tired man snored as he rode down the conveyer belt and was dumped into a giant vat of sticky bubblegum. It took 14 workers and 12 firefighters to pry Mr. Crawford out from the mess.

After this unfortunate incident, Mr. Crawford realized he needed an extra set of hands to help out at home. He scoured newspapers and the Internet in search of someone who was qualified to take care of his house and his young son. After interviewing many nice old ladies, Mr. Crawford hired a woman named Agnes Blackwood.

Judging from her list of prior accomplishments, one might think Agnes was Mary Poppins herself! According to her resume, she had

1. graduated at the top of her class from the International University of Nannies;

2. taken care of the vice president of the United States' children;

3. broken a world record for changing a diaper, scrubbing a bathroom floor, and preparing a seven-course meal—all in under one minute.

Oh, yes, and Agnes also had several impressive recommendations from past employers. They included the Queen of England, Gandhi, and Santa Claus.

Even though her claims were somewhat outrageous, Mr. Crawford was much too tired to check Agnes's references. He felt that any help was good enough at this point. So, soon Agnes moved in, and Mr. Crawford went to sleep.

"I can't thank you enough for coming to help us out," Mr. Crawford told Agnes in between yawns. "I'm sure it won't be for (yawn) very long—just enough time to get me back on my feet (yawn) and adjusted to the change."

Five months turned into six months, and then six months turned into one year.... Now eight years had passed. By this time Mr. Crawford had graduated from the assembly line, the house was so clean it practically cleaned itself, and Jason was 10 years old and too grown up to need a nanny. But Agnes was still around...and Jason hated it.

There were two sides to Agnes, and only Jason got to see them both. When Mr. Crawford was home, Agnes was charming and kind. She'd gently say things to Jason like, "Yes, dear, of course you may have another cookie! A growing boy needs to eat!" This was always followed by a loving pinch on the cheek. But when Mr. Crawford was away on one of his business trips, Agnes morphed into an evil witch and constantly scolded Jason. "Get your paws out of that cookie jar, you spoiled, rotten little urchin!" she'd yell. Or, "The next time I have to tell you to take a bath, you'll be hearing it underwater!" These rants were always followed by a rough pinch to Jason's arm.

In Jason's opinion, Agnes could be best described as a human praying mantis. She was tall and thin with sharp bony features and piercing dark eyes. When his father was away, Jason feared that one night Agnes might raise her insect limbs and gobble him up in his sleep.

Jason had tried to tell his father about the way Agnes acted, but by the time Mr. Crawford returned home from one of his trips, she was always back to her phony, sugary sweet ways.

"Jason was just a doll while you were away, weren't you, you little angel?" she'd say as she tugged affectionately on Jason's ear (just a bit too hard).

Jason really didn't deserve this kind of treatment; he was a very good boy. He got decent grades at school and had good manners. The only thing that seemed to concern some people—especially his teachers—was his overactive imagination.

Jason was a daydreamer, as all children can be, but his imagination had a tendency to go a bit too wild. Jason's teachers believed that his daydreaming interfered with his learning and affected his sense of reality. One afternoon in math class, Jason fantasized that he'd turned into a giant pterodactyl. Soon he was flapping the tiny wings on his back and flying out of the window and into the clouds. You probably can guess what happened next. Let's just say that Jason was very lucky his classroom was located on the first floor. It's no wonder his teachers believed that it was unhealthy to daydream so much.

Jason's constant daydreaming infuriated Agnes, who had about as much imagination as a housefly. She was mired deep in practicality and probably hadn't smiled or laughed since pterodactyls roamed the earth. Jason wasn't sure why he daydreamed so much. Perhaps it was the only way he could escape the harsh reality of living with Agnes.

One evening Jason knew he was in trouble. At the dinner table, Mr. Crawford announced that the gum factory was going to send him to Japan for the summer and that Jason and Agnes would have to manage without him for three whole months. Jason begged and pleaded with his father to stay home. He warned of giant lizards that breathed fire and destroyed Japanese cities with their bare hands. But it was no use—later that week his father was on an airplane, leaving Jason alone with Agnes.

Which brings us to the last straw....

It was a bright summer morning. Jason and Oliver Jensen, the boy who lived next door, were trying to think of something to do to pass the time. It was Oliver who had suggested they build a wooden cart with wheels, take it to the top of Hickory Hill, and ride it all the way down to the bottom. Jason absolutely loved this idea! He began to imagine that he and his friend were world-famous astronauts being sent on a mission to save the galaxy.

Quickly the two boys got to work. They gathered boards and nails and then hammered, sanded, and painted their two-seated cart a beautiful bright blue. On either side of the cart, Oliver wrote in big white letters: I Luv Fun. After the paint had dried, they attached the wheels of Oliver's sister's roller skates to the bottom of the cart. With this finishing touch, the boys were ready to ride their cart down the hill.

Wearing bicycle helmets and swim goggles, the boys proudly stood next to their rickety wooden cart at the top of Hickory Hill. Oliver took the front seat, and Jason climbed into the back.

"Ready for take-off?" Oliver asked in a deep, official-sounding voice.

"All systems go!" announced Jason, equally official-sounding. He pretended to rev up the engine, and with that, Oliver leaned forward, and they were off!

At first the cart started down the hill slowly, but it gathered momentum. Soon the vehicle was speeding down the slope, creaking and swerving and gaining more speed. Jason and Oliver held on to the sides of the cart, laughing and screaming as the wind pulled at their cheeks. Jason had already escaped into a whole other world. He was imagining that he was blasting enemy spacecraft in his mission to save the galaxy. But suddenly something caused him to snap back to reality. At almost the same time as Oliver did, Jason realized that there was one tiny problem with their cart—it had no brakes!

Oliver began screaming. Jason kicked his foot out to slow them down, but the cart just skidded roughly against the dirt path and scraped Jason's ankle. There was nothing they could do. Defeated, Jason closed his eyes, held his breath, and awaited their fate.

The boys hit the bottom of the hill with a thump and careened into traffic. Jason still had his eyes closed and he heard screeching tires, honking horns, and the sound of metal crashing against metal. Bravely Jason opened one eye. Then he screamed. The cart was heading straight for the window of Mr. Carter's Hair Salon! The boys both jumped out of the cart and tumbled roughly onto the sidewalk. The last thing Jason heard was the sound of shattering glass. Then everything went black.

Jason woke up in a hospital bed. He had a bandaged wrist and a thumping headache. Staring down at him were a doctor, a police officer, and Agnes. Oliver lay moaning in the bed next to Jason, his leg wrapped in a full cast. Mrs. Jensen was perched above her son like a watchful bird, smoothing his hair and cooing words of endearment.

The doctor leaned down and shone a light in Jason's eyes. "Look to the left," he said.

Jason did.

"Look to the right."

Jason did.

"Okay. It's nothing too serious," the doctor announced. "Just a sprained wrist and a bump on the head. He's ready to go home." And with that the doctor closed his folder and left the room.

Jason could feel Agnes's eyes burning into his flesh, but he refused to look at her. He knew the only reason Agnes hadn't gobbled him up yet was because there was a police officer in the

room.

"Well, son, it looks like you have a lot of explaining to do," Officer Toalson said sternly, smoothing his thick mustache and then crossing his arms in a menacing stance.

"It was—we didn't mean to—" Jason began, but he found he couldn't get the words out. Jason glanced over just in time to see Oliver looking at him from the corner of one eye. His friend quickly shut his eyes and continued moaning.

"You are extremely lucky that no one was hurt, but the damages to property that you two caused was serious," the police officer explained. "That's $2,000 worth of damage to Mr. Buonomo's new car, $500 for a new window at Mr. Carter's Hair Salon, and $75 to Mrs. Pennywick, who received quite an unfortunate haircut at the time of the collision. The poor woman looks like a half-shaved poodle!"

Jason gulped. He still felt Agnes's eyes burning through his skin.

"Your nanny here was kind enough to pay the bill," the policeman said, turning to Agnes, who smiled sweetly at him and shrugged modestly.

"She's not my nanny," Jason cringed. He told Agnes numerous times before that he was embarrassed when she called herself his "nanny." He was too old for one! But Agnes took any chance she had to make him feel awkward.

"I hope you boys have learned a valuable lesson from all of this," the policeman continued. "Now whose brilliant idea was it to build that contraption and take it down the hill?"

Oliver let out a loud dramatic moan. Jason looked at him and scowled. "It was both of our ideas, sir," Jason said softly. "We're really sorry."

Agnes cleared her throat. "If I may interrupt, Officer Toalson, sir," she said meekly. "I'm sure that Jason is very, very sorry for his actions. He really is a wonderfully behaved little boy. I can assure you that something like this will never happen again."

Officer Toalson smiled warmly at Agnes. "I'm sure you'll do the best you can, dear. Jason is quite lucky to have such a wonderful nanny like yourself." Then he turned to Jason and said, "Since you're only 10 years old and have no prior convictions, and since Nanny here has been so sweet," he added, winking at Agnes, "I won't add this incident to your permanent record. I only hope that you will stay out of trouble from now on."

"I will, sir. Thank you," said Jason.

And with that Officer Toalson tipped his hat and left the room.

Agnes took Jason through the checkout procedure at the hospital, acting like a concerned, caring nanny by making a point to fuss over his bruises in front of all the nurses. She thanked everyone profusely, and with her arm gripped tightly around Jason's shoulders, she led him out of the emergency room's doors and into the waiting car.

It wasn't until they'd rode out of the parking lot, driven three blocks, and were clear of all witnesses that Agnes pulled over to the side of the road. She turned toward Jason and glared at him. Rage was in her eyes. "THIS...IS...THE *LAST STRAW*!" she screamed.

"But—I—" he stuttered.

"Don't you interrupt me, you disrespectful, UNGRATEFUL LITTLE BRAT!" she yelled. Her pointy face was red and flecks of spit flew from her mouth.

"But Agnes! We were just pretending to be astronauts!" Jason pleaded. "I'm sorry!"

"JUST WAIT UNTIL I TELL YOUR FATHER ABOUT ALL OF

THIS—ALL THE MONEY YOU JUST COST HIM BECAUSE OF YOUR STUPIDITY AND YOUR RIDICULOUSLY FANTASTIC IMAGINATION. DON'T YOU *DARE* SPEAK OUT OF TURN!"

"It was an accident!"

"THERE ARE NO MORE ACCIDENTS! YOU'VE DONE IT THIS TIME! I WON'T SPEND MY ENTIRE SUMMER WITH SUCH A DISOBEDIENT BOY!" Agnes screeched, banging her fists on the dashboard.

"But I—wait...what?" Jason asked, his heart skipping a beat. Not having to spend the summer with Agnes would be a reward, not a punishment!

"I've decided to send you away," Agnes said, calming down for a moment. She was gripping the steering wheel so tightly that her bony knuckles had turned white. "You will go to a place where they'll teach you the true meaning of good behavior!" She dug into her purse and retrieved an envelope that she thrust angrily at Jason. "It's a place where they'll teach you to respect your elders, learn to be cooperative, improve your work ethic, and help you accept REALITY!" Agnes continued angrily.

Jason pulled the letter out of the envelope and read it.

> Dear Parent/Guardian:
>
> Do you often find yourself losing patience with your child? Have you experienced headaches, muscle cramps, or fits of tears due to an unruly tyke? Do you find yourself imagining what your life would be like without the constant anxiety and struggle that comes with raising an out-of-control youngster? Well, worry no more. We have the answer for you.

Located in scenic Fog Valley, *Von Ulf's Retreat for Unruly Youths* caters to the needs of spoiled and undisciplined children. Here at *Von Ulf's*, we offer a unique treatment plan developed especially with your child's best interest in mind. For more details, call 555-VON-ULFS.

Sincerely,

Isaac Von Ulf

Isaac Von Ulf
Owner and Head of Discipline
at *Von Ulf's Retreat for Unruly Youths*

At the bottom of the page, underneath the signature, there was a small jagged line of unreadable ink. At the top right corner, there was a picture of Isaac Von Ulf leaning against a tree. The severe-looking man had wild, wavy blond hair. His eyes were black, and a small white scar cut through his left eyebrow. His thin lips were pursed in a frown. Mr. Von Ulf looked like a man who didn't smile very often.

Jason could barely believe this was happening. *Go away for the summer...to some camp for bad kids? This is ridiculous!* he thought. Jason wasn't a spoiled or undisciplined child—he was good! It was Agnes who was unreasonable! Angrily he crumpled up the letter and shoved it into the front pocket of his jeans. Jason had a feeling there was nothing he could say that would make Agnes change her mind. After all, it had been the last straw.

Chapter Two

The Bus Ride

On less than a week, Jason was packed and ready to go to Von Ulf's Retreat for Unruly Youths. Jason lugged his suitcase outside and glanced next door. Still in a full leg cast, Oliver Jensen was lounging on the swing on his front porch and playing a handheld video game. The new puppy his mother had surprised him with was yipping and jumping excitedly, and his little sister, Tibby, was drawing on his cast. The front door swung open and Mrs. Jensen appeared, carrying a tray of strawberry ice cream.

"Thanks, Mumsy!" said Oliver, taking the tray.

"Of course, dear. You've been through so much," she said, chuckling warmly.

"Could you bring Mr. Fluffington a bone, Mumsy?" asked Oliver, pointing to the puppy.

Jason felt Agnes's knee nudge him in the back and he stumbled down the steps. "Get moving, you rotten thing! If you miss that bus, don't even think about coming back here!" she said, slamming the door behind him.

Jason sighed and continued towards the curb.

"Hi, Jason!" Oliver called, waving from his swing. "Where are you going?"

"Never mind," Jason called back. "Just enjoy your ice cream and your new dog." He had been a little upset with Oliver ever since the cart incident. It had been Oliver's idea all along to build the cart and ride it down Hickory Hill. Yet when it came time to confess, he'd told his mother and Officer Toalson that it had been all Jason's idea and that he'd just gone along with it. Now according to Mrs. Jensen, Jason was "that-no-good-troublemaker-next-door-who-stole-Tibby's-roller-skates!"

Jason ignored Oliver and focused his attention on the corner, where a yellow school bus had appeared and was headed towards him. Painted in red lettering on its sides were the words *Von Ulf's Retreat*. The bus rattled to a stop in front of the curb, and its creaky doors swung open. A hunchbacked old man with a deeply wrinkled face sat behind the steering wheel. His eyes were puffy, and he wore a nametag on his shirt that said Wally. He scowled at Jason, and with an impatient wave, motioned for him to get on the bus.

Jason climbed up the stairs. Immediately he was met with a chorus of boos and hisses. The bus was filled with children of all ages, half of them standing or kneeling on their seats while throwing things at one another and shouting. As Jason made his way toward the back of the bus, a bulldogish boy with a red crew cut stuck out his foot and tripped him, causing Jason to lurch forward into the open seat behind the large boy. This elicited laughter and hooting from the other children.

Jason sunk into his seat as the bus pulled away. A young boy about his age sat slumped down low next to him, clutching a duffel bag on his lap. The boy had blond hair and glasses and was wearing a red hooded sweatshirt that had a big yellow stain on the front. He looked at Jason and said quietly, "They did the same thing to me."

"Oh yeah?" said Jason, ducking as an apple core whizzed past his head.

The boy nodded. "That one tripped me," he explained, pointing to the bulldog in front of them, who was now twisting the arm of a scrawny girl sitting next to him. "And they all yelled at me and called me names until the next person got on the bus. Just be glad they ran out of mustard by the time you got here." He pointed glumly to the stain on his sweatshirt.

To Jason, there seemed to be something different about the boy sitting next to him. He wasn't like the others on the bus, who acted more like a pack of wild animals than say, a boy whose fake-nanny had sent him away to a behavior retreat because he had an overactive imagination.

"My name is Miles Sheldon," said the boy.

"I'm Jason Crawford." Then, after removing a sticky wad of wet paper that had somehow appeared on his sleeve, he asked, "Why are you here?"

"My parents are teaching me a lesson about stealing," he sighed, "even though I didn't steal anything. Another boy in my class stole money from our teacher's purse and hid it in my desk."

"And your parents didn't believe you?" Jason asked, stunned.

"No, they're very strict. They tend to believe anyone besides me these days," Miles said. "Why are you here?"

"It's a long story," Jason sighed.

A voice from above interrupted them. "Hey nerds," said the bulldog, leaning over the seat and peering down at them with squinty eyes. He was cracking his fat, bruised knuckles and wearing a sneer on his face. "My name is Boris Stubbs. Remember that name because for the rest of the summer, I'm in charge. If you want to get on my good side, you'll pay me a dollar a day for protection, starting right now."

"I'm not interested," said Jason, straightening up in his seat. "And he isn't either," Jason added, motioning towards Miles, who had slouched down even further.

Boris's jowls hung low as he scowled and cracked his knuckles again. "I don't think you understood me. I said...*I'm in charge*. I've been to these types of places before. They can get pretty rough. Wimps like you need protection," he said.

At this point the scrawny girl sitting next to Boris stuck her head over the seat, too. She had long, stringy brown hair, freckles, dark circles under her eyes, and a nasty look on her face. Jason imagined that Agnes must have looked just like her as a child.

"What's going on, Boris?" the girl asked in a nasally voice.

"These two here have decided not to pay the protection fee this summer," Boris said.

The girl broke out into a fit of cackles, revealing two cracked front teeth. "Good. More boxing practice for you, then!" she howled. "They look like two perfect punching bags to me!"

"This is my new secretary, Fern Pratt. You can pay her when you're ready," said Boris, pointing at the girl. "The sooner the better. Trust me."

"I told you, we're not paying you anything," said Jason. He usually got along with everyone at school, so he didn't have much experience with bullies. But he wasn't about to give into threats now. Miles, however, seemed scared. Jason could see his hands trembling as he reached into his bag and took out a dollar.

"Miles, don't," said Jason.

Before he could say anything else, Fern ripped the dollar out of Miles's hand.

"Ha ha!" she said.

"Give it back to him you thief!" yelled Jason.

"Finders keepers!" mocked Fern, handing the dollar to Boris.

Jason rose from his seat. Huge Boris stood up, too. The big bully stood a whole foot taller than Jason. All of the children on the bus turned their attention to the two boys, who were now staring coldly at each other. Then they began chanting, "Fight, fight, fight!" Fern was screaming the loudest.

"You've got some nerve for such a little runt," scoffed Boris.

From up front Wally the bus driver could see what was happening. "Sit down!" he yelled in a croaky voice that sounded like an old toad. "Mr. Von Ulf will not be pleased if I have to report you two before you even arrive at the retreat!"

Boris was obviously someone who didn't listen to his elders. Secretly Jason was terrified, but he knew that he couldn't back down now, even if it meant...POW! Boris's fist met Jason's nose. A sharp pain followed the punch and sent Jason falling back into his seat. The bus erupted with laughter and taunts. Jason's eyes watered as he clutched his nose and watched Boris and Fern laughing above him.

"You can get used to that kind of thing every day," cautioned Boris, before finally turning around and focusing his attention on another boy who had just boarded the bus.

Jason was in shock. He had never been punched in the face.

"Are you okay?" asked Miles worriedly. "You should've just given him a dollar."

"No way," said Jason, still clutching his nose. "I'm fine. It's not broken or bleeding or anything."

The yellow school bus continued driving into the night, through one town and into the next. The sky was dark, and a bright, nearly full moon shone overhead. Jason's nose throbbed. He stared out the window as the bus rolled over hills and passed cornfields. The kids on the bus had calmed down a bit, although there were still some outbursts of kicking and screaming followed by name-calling, hair pulling, and warnings from Wally.

As he looked out the window, Jason caught his reflection in

the glass. His dark wavy hair was messy, his brown eyes were bloodshot, and his newly punched nose looked puffy and swollen. *What a great way to start my summer*, he thought.

"Where are we, anyway?" asked Miles.

"I have no idea," replied Jason, feeling the bump on his nose with his fingers. "I've never even heard of Fog Valley."

"Nobody has," said Miles. "It's not on any map, that's for sure. I did some research."

"Yeah, Agnes just got some letter in the mail and decided to send me," said Jason. "The picture of that Isaac Von Ulf guy sure looks creepy, huh?"

"This is all so unfair," said Miles gloomily.

"I know," agreed Jason, staring out the window again.

The bus turned onto a dirt path that led into a forest. Tall pine trees surrounded them, blocking out the moonlight. It became darker and darker as the bus traveled deeper into the woods. After some time the bus slowed down and came to a stop.

Wally stood up and turned to the group. "Grab your things. I want everyone in a single file line behind me. No pushing or shoving or talking as we get off the bus."

Everyone eventually exited the bus, but there wasn't anything single file or quiet about it. There was a lot of jostling for position, and most children were pushed, causing them to come tumbling down the steps in a disorderly heap. This resulted in more pushing, grabbing, and yelling. A few children even squeezed out of the bus through its windows.

Once outside, Jason saw that they were at the base of a large mountain. A tunnel had been cut through the rocks, and a number of wooden carts were waiting on a track that led into the dark passageway. As on the exterior of the bus, the words *Von Ulf's*

Retreat were painted in red on the sides of each cart.

The forest was alive with nighttime noises; there were croaking frogs, hooting owls, and howling coyotes in the distance. Jason felt uneasy. Judging from the looks on some of the other kids' faces, and the sudden silence that befell the group, he wasn't the only one who felt this way.

"What's the meaning of this?" an immaculate looking boy with perfectly styled hair demanded. He clutched a designer suitcase and wore a spotless white jacket with his family crest sewn onto the lapel.

Wally ignored the boy and directed the children to take a seat in the carts and strap themselves in with the seat belts. "Keep your hands in the cart at all times, and do not undo your strap," he instructed.

Jason swallowed the lump of fear that had risen in his throat and imagined that he was merely preparing to get on a roller coaster at the amusement park.

"My parents will not be pleased to hear that I had to travel through a dirty mountain on an unsafe conveyance," complained the boy in white, crossing his arms defiantly.

"Just get in the cart!" hollered Wally. "Your parents can take it up with Mr. Von Ulf!"

Jason and Miles sat down next to each other and buckled their seatbelts. There was a lot of protesting, and the general mood was a mix of fear and nervousness. Some of the kids tried to maintain their cool by making wisecracks and laughing anxiously. Two carts ahead of Jason and Miles, Boris Stubbs was still in bully mode. He had the boy in front of him in a headlock and was rubbing his knuckles roughly into the poor child's scalp. Obviously Boris was not too concerned about where the carts were going.

The boy with the perfect hair draped a towel over his seat before sitting down and continued to moan about the "audacity of it all" and how "Father is going to sue the whole world and everyone in it...."

Meanwhile Wally made sure that everyone was strapped in the carts. Then he turned around and walked quickly back towards the bus.

"Wait a minute!" a large, red-faced girl in the last cart called out to him. "Aren't you coming with us?"

Wally turned around and an unmistakable look of fear filled his eyes. "Come with you?" he said. "You must be crazy! I wouldn't be caught *dead* where you're headed!" And with that he scurried onto the bus and hastily pulled away.

At the exact same time, the train of carts suddenly surged forward and began moving along the track and into the mountain.

Chapter Three

That's No Fish!

The only sound Jason heard as they entered the tunnel were the carts' wheels grinding steadily along the tracks. Inside the mountain it was dark and cold, and it smelled of earth. Jason could now hear the sound of water trickling down the walls. He gripped the sides of his cart, trying to stay calm, and wondered what Wally had meant when he'd said, "I wouldn't be caught dead where you're headed." More importantly Jason wondered, *Where exactly were they headed?* Judging from the shade of green that Miles's face had turned, Jason knew his new friend must have been wondering the same thing.

Suddenly, from somewhere within the walls of the mountain, a woman's voice echoed from invisible speakers:

"You are about to enter Fog Valley, home of the legendary Von Ulfs's Retreat for Unruly Youths," the voice intoned. "The inhabitants of Fog Valley are proud to host the world's most successful reform camp, led by the legendary Isaac Von Ulf. Mr. Von Ulf believes that no child, regardless of his or her poor attitude and bad habits, is a lost cause, and that all are capable of reform. The inhabitants of the retreat will be taught respect, cooperation, and discipline. At the end of the stay, all inhabitants will leave Fog Valley with a new appreciation of life and a complete understanding of acceptable behavior."

Just then both the voice and the carts stopped abruptly. The silence was deafening. *Thump, thump, thump....* Jason could hear his heart pounding through his chest. He was about to say something to Miles, when all of a sudden the carts lurched forward. Jason felt his stomach drop to the floor as they headed down a steep decline. Everyone began screaming as the carts accelerated. Jason felt as if he was speeding down Hickory Hill all over again; but then *whish*, the carts made a sharp turn and headed upwards and then *whish*, they went down again. Up and down, left and right; Jason now felt almost as if they were on an extreme roller coaster ride. But it was terrifying because in the blackness of the tunnel he couldn't see a thing. Jason held his breath and closed his eyes tight, praying for the ride to end.

Suddenly Jason felt as if everything was moving in slow motion. A blinding flash lit up the darkness for a split second, and he heard a loud steady *beep...beep...beep....* Then he heard the woman's voice over the speakers again. "Breathe...," the voice said.

Jason did. As he exhaled, the carts leveled off and emerged from the mountain, coming to a halt. Everyone was gasping for air. Some children were crying from fear, others were laughing with relief, and a few even threw up over the sides of the carts. Jason was shaking, and Miles was hunched over, clutching his knees, afraid to open his eyes.

"Miles, we're here," whispered Jason, his voice cracking.

Miles slowly looked up.

They were in another forest. Most of the children were looking around fearfully—not sure what to expect next. Waiting for them by the carts were three dwarfs in matching black clothes. Bald, stocky, and wearing frowns, the three pint-sized beings—who must have been identical triplets—didn't seem to be a very friendly welcoming committee. After everyone had climbed out of the carts, Jason watched as one of the dwarfs held out a small electronic device and pointed it towards the hole in the mountain.

He clicked it once, causing a lever high above the tunnel to turn. Then the carts moved backwards into the mountain, and a heavy wooden gate slowly closed over the opening, shutting them in for the summer.

In silence, the dwarfs led the nervous group of children through the woods until they reached a clearing. The eerie sound of frogs croaking and crickets chirping filled the air. Ahead of them was a lake blanketed by a layer of thick fog. Jason couldn't see more than a few yards in front of him. *I guess now we know why it's called Fog Valley*, he thought.

The dwarfs divided the children into three groups and then directed each group to a large raft that was waiting on the shore. Jason and Miles were ushered onto a raft with six other children: two moody brothers, who wouldn't stop arguing; a girl named Yolanda Jones, who had accidentally burned down her neighbor's garage; a boy named Pedro Lopez, who had stolen his parents' car and crashed it into a mailbox; a pint-sized six-year-old named Robby Bowman, who refused to eat anything but candy; and Thelma Butterworth, the large, red-faced girl who had asked Wally if he was coming with them.

Once Jason's group was situated on the raft, one of the dwarfs joined them and announced in a gruff voice, "Everyone grab an oar and start paddling on my count."

Jason and Miles each picked up a heavy oar and dipped it into the water. The two brothers fought over the same oar. It took a while, but finally everyone was in sync and soon they were gliding across the foggy black water. Once they were about 10 yards out into the lake, Thelma Butterworth decided she was done rowing and would rather eat a chocolate bar that she'd stashed in her pocket.

The dwarf noticed Thelma and scolded, "Put down that candy and start rowing! This isn't a luxury cruise!"

"I don't feel like it!" Thelma said, taking a bite of her chocolate and crossing her chubby arms. She had short black hair, green eyes, and a red, flushed face.

"I don't want to have to tell Mr. Von Ulf that you were misbehaving so soon into your stay," warned the dwarf.

Thelma pursed her lips defiantly and pointed to her T-shirt. It was pink and about three sizes too small. On it there was a picture of a cat with a paint bucket on its head, and the words below it said: *Ask me if I care!*

"You don't care?" the dwarf asked without blinking an eye. "Then get off the raft."

"No way! We're in the middle of a lake and I can't swim!" Thelma cried loudly.

"Then row," said the dwarf. "I can guarantee you, you won't survive what's in that lake—whether you can swim or not."

Thelma's eyes widened. "Why? What's in the lake?" she asked, gulping.

"Just row," said the dwarf.

Jason and Miles exchanged worried glances.

Thelma shoved the rest of the chocolate bar into her mouth, blew air out her nostrils, and reluctantly picked up her oar.

"Fine, but we better get a full dinner. I've barely eaten anything today, and I feel weak from all this work," Thelma whined.

Jason looked across the lake at the two other rafts. He could hear the well-dressed boy still complaining. "This is an outrage!" he was yelling. "I'm not meant to do hard labor. At home we have servants to do this kind of thing!" But his complaints fell on deaf ears, and at one point someone on his raft pulled a slimy weed from the lake and threw it onto his white jacket.

When Boris and Fern's raft glided past, Boris called out to Jason, "How's your nose, nerd?"

Fern cackled loudly and splashed water towards Jason using her oar. Jason saw that the others on the raft were all huddled together away from Boris, and most of them already had black eyes.

It was then, from somewhere ahead of them, that Jason heard a loud splash. For a split second, he could see through the fog—two long, black tentacles with suction cups were flailing above the surface of the water. Then, to his horror, a creature with one huge black eye poked its head out from the water for just a moment and then slunk quickly back under the surface.

"What was that?" Jason screamed.

"What was what?" the dwarf asked.

"That...that...*thing* in the water!"

"What *thing*?"

"That...that *creature*! It just popped out...and it..." Jason tried to find the words, but he was still in shock. The other children stopped rowing and looked around curiously.

"It must have been a fish," said the dwarf calmly.

"That was no fish," Jason insisted. "That was a...a...sea monster or something!"

"Don't let your imagination run away from you," cautioned the dwarf.

"Miles, did you see it?"

"No," said Miles, wiping the fog off his glasses. "What was it?"

"I—I don't know...it was..." Jason stuttered, straining his eyes to catch another glimpse of the thing. *Had he been the only one to see it?* Nobody else seemed to have noticed.

"QUIET DOWN AND KEEP ROWING!" yelled the dwarf. "When we reach our destination, Mr. Von Ulf will explain all you need to know about the inhabitants of the lake!"

Everyone was silent. A feeling of anxiety fell over the group, and the only sound was the oars dipping into the black water.

"Something's not right," said Jason quietly.

"What do you mean?" asked Miles.

"That thing in the water...it wasn't a fish!" Jason insisted, shaking his head from side to side. "It had long tentacles and one huge eye!"

"Maybe it was an octopus," Miles shrugged.

"Octopuses don't live in *lakes*, Miles," said Jason. "And another thing, why did the lady on the loudspeaker keep calling the people in town and at the camp 'inhabitants'? Why didn't she just call them...well...*people*?"

"I don't get your point," said Miles.

"And the dwarf used the word 'inhabitants,' too, when I asked what lived in the lake," Jason said.

As they neared the shore, Jason heard the unmistakable sound of wolves howling from inside the surrounding forest. Through the fog and trees, he could see lights shining from a cluster of cabins nestled up in the mountains.

"Cool," cried Yolanda Jones, "we're going camping! Can we start a bonfire?"

"It looks scary," said little Robby Bowman, sucking on a piece of licorice.

"Hey, Mr. Dwarf. How come he built the place way up in the mountains?" asked Pedro Lopez.

The dwarf looked at Pedro and very calmly replied, "Why to

keep you in of course." And then he added, sending a cold chill down Jason's spine, "And to keep everything else out!"

Chapter Four

Monsters Everywhere

The dwarfs directed the children off the rafts and led them up a winding path. The higher they climbed, the better view they had of the valley below. Clusters of pine trees blanketed the sides of an enormous mountain range that surrounded the valley on all four sides. Through breaks in the fog, Jason could see the rooftops of houses in the town below. Their red brick chimneys and thatched roofs gave the valley a quaint, cozy feeling.

"Everyone remain in a single file and stay on the path," one of the dwarfs instructed. "Don't push each other or stray into the woods. It's not safe, and I won't be held accountable for what happens to you if you don't listen."

The first thing Jason saw once they reached the camp was a large wooden sign arching across two poles with the words *Von Ulf's Retreat for Unruly Youths* painted on it in red letters. In the camp itself, several large log cabins were surrounded by rows and rows of smaller cabins. These smaller log cabins each had big numbers on their doors and torches placed in sconces above the windows. The dwarfs explained that the children would sleep in the smaller cabins and that the larger cabins were facilities, which included the Kitchen and Mess Hall, administration buildings, the Infirmary, learning centers, and a stable.

"Horseback riding!" Jason said to Miles excitedly. "This is starting to seem more like a vacation than a punishment!"

The group gathered around the main cabin and chatted enthusiastically until the door swung open. A man with wild eyes and long blond hair stood in the doorway. He was leaning on a long wooden walking stick. Jason recognized the man from the picture on the letter: it was Isaac Von Ulf, the owner and head disciplinarian of the retreat.

"Welcome to my retreat," Von Ulf began, in a low and somber voice. "Congratulations for making it across the lake in one piece. The Kraken can be rather unfriendly to visitors." He said this very matter-of-factly, as if someone had merely asked him what color the sky was.

Jason nudged Miles, who was staring wide-eyed at Von Ulf and looking as if he'd just swallowed something very sour. "I told you it wasn't a fish," Jason whispered from the corner of his mouth.

Someone in the back blurted out the question that everyone wanted answered. "What's a kraken?"

"I'd really rather you didn't interrupt me. It's a very bad habit," Von Ulf said, shaking his head. "But since you asked, a Kraken is a 12-limbed, one-eyed water dweller that has a taste for human flesh. You'll find that it won't bother you as long as you stay away from the water. So for those of you who may have grand illusions of escaping the retreat, consider yourself warned."

The children were stunned into silence, but after a few seconds Boris piped up. "Pshaw," he grunted loudly, crossing his beefy arms and looking around. "He's just saying that to scare us. There's no such thing as a kraken."

"Isn't there?" asked Von Ulf.

"Nope! I don't believe you!" answered Boris, shaking his watermelon head.

"Suit yourself," said Von Ulf. "But if you decide to take a dip in the lake, better tuck in your limbs!"

Boris rolled his eyes and mumbled something about not being

afraid. However, he was noticeably quieter after Von Ulf's warning.

"Excuse me," said the boy in the white jacket as he pushed his way to the front. "My name is Chadwick Wellington XVII. My father, who's a very influential citizen, will be quite upset to learn that you lied to us and tried to frighten us. He won't approve of your scare tactics. Now, I demand to be shown to my room!"

"Let me ask you something, son," Von Ulf began. "Why do you think your father sent you here?"

"My father sent me here merely because he and my mother wanted to go skiing in Switzerland alone this year. There is no behavioral issue with me. I can assure you of that!" Chadwick stated rather snobbishly.

"Tsk, tsk," said Von Ulf. "It seems that your father sent you here because you are spoiled and speak out of turn. Spend a few months with me and we'll clear that little problem right up!"

"But I—" Chadwick began.

"Now if all of you are done interrupting me," Von Ulf continued, his eyes scanning the crowd of children, "then I will give you a brief overview of Fog Valley's history."

Jason didn't know what to think. He knew that what he'd seen in the lake wasn't normal, but could what Von Ulf had said be true? Krakens were sea monsters of myth, and Jason had read about the giant squid-like creature in many adventure books. They couldn't be real, though...*could they?* Even Jason, with his "overactive imagination," knew that krakens didn't truly exist.

Von Ulf proceeded with his history lesson and began explaining how he'd come to choose Fog Valley for the location of his retreat.

"I am an explorer by profession, you see," he said. "Years ago I was looking for a place to set up my behavioral retreat, a dream of mine for many years. While I was traveling on one of my geographic expeditions, I accidentally stumbled upon Fog Valley. What I found here amazed me." He paused. "Can anyone guess what I found?"

At this point the group was very curious and very confused. Von Ulf certainly had everyone's full attention. Well, almost everyone's....

"What did you find? Your brain?" Boris shouted. This comment was followed by Fern's obnoxious cackle.

Von Ulf's black eyes narrowed into little slits, and he glared at Boris for what seemed like an eternity. It was a terrifying stare and even Jason felt sorry for Boris. Without Von Ulf having to say a word, Boris quickly shut his mouth and looked down at his feet.

Von Ulf continued. "I found that the entrance to Fog Valley is located upon the exact coordinates whereby fantasy meets reality. Every fantastical being you've ever dreamed of or read about resides here in Fog Valley...every single one." He paused. All eyes in the group widened, and all jaws dropped.

"I couldn't believe it myself at first," Von Ulf chuckled. "So I figured that this would be the *perfect* place to set up my retreat for undisciplined children. What better way is there to teach children manners than by scaring the living daylights out of them? Or to have them learn to respect others' differences than by living with those who are different than themselves? Fog Valley seemed like the perfect setting for a camp to make children understand cooperation and the importance of adapting to new and strange environments.

"Well, at first my plan was going along just swimmingly—almost too swimmingly, in fact. After my first year, the valley's inhabitants—the fantastical beings that made their homes here—

started to catch on to its success, and they began sending their troubled children here as well!"

The silence was almost deafening at this point.

"You mean...?" Thelma finally blurted out.

"Exactly. You'll be meeting all kinds of children here with problems just like yours," said Von Ulf. "And you'll learn that the basic principles you follow in order to survive in your world—respect, cooperation, and discipline—are the same basic principles for survival in every world. If you learn to embrace these character traits, you will take valuable lessons back home with you."

"And what if we don't?" asked Pedro Lopez.

"Then you won't," said Von Ulf, raising his scarred eyebrow.

Won't what? Go home? Jason thought. There were a million questions running through his mind.

"Oh, look, here they come now," said Von Ulf, smiling and motioning towards the valley.

In the distance below, Jason could see another group of children exiting a bus and forming an unorganized line, much like their own group had done. He couldn't see what these new children looked like until they lumbered up the path towards them, led by three more identical dwarfs. It was then that Jason got the shock of his life. They *were* children alright, but not like any children he'd ever seen before.

These kids were monsters—real monsters. They were growling, spitting, hissing, and groaning. One was a girl with long slithery snakes coming from her head. Another was a boy covered almost entirely from head to toe in shaggy white fur. There was a creature that was dripping wet and covered with seaweed and looked as if it had just emerged from a filthy swamp. Another child had horns coming from his head, and some of the others had claws, fangs,

talons, wings, and yellow eyes.

Jason's feet were rooted in place. He felt numb and lightheaded and thought he might faint from shock. Miles had done just that. One of the dwarfs promptly splashed water on Miles's face and then dragged him off to the Infirmary.

"Children from the Other Side, meet your equals from Fog Valley," Von Ulf announced, motioning to the newcomers. "I do hope you can all get along," he added with a smirk.

A boy with the features of a wolf suddenly lunged from the line and went straight for Fern Pratt. He would have reached her if one of the dwarfs hadn't stepped in between them, brandishing a long metal stick and keeping him at bay. The wolf-boy growled and flashed his yellow fangs at Fern, which sent her screaming and cowering behind Boris, who suddenly didn't seem so tough.

"Tsk, tsk...Mordico. Back again this year?" asked Von Ulf in a bored tone. The boy just growled and barked back at him. All Jason could do was stare in shock. He tried to remember what would've been so bad about a summer spent alone with Agnes.

Chapter Five

Creepy Cabin #13

After a few more fainting outbreaks and skirmishes between the humans and the monster children, Von Ulf got down to business. He assured the group that he wouldn't tolerate disobedience or bad tempers from anyone, and was determined to keep the promise that he had made to their parents: their child would return home 100 percent reformed. Von Ulf also made it clear that if he had to see someone in his office for repeated offenses, it would *not* be a good thing. He also stressed that although he wouldn't be around all the time, he had many staff members who would ensure that rules such as these were followed: (1) children must not leave their cabins after dark unless escorted by a discipline leader; (2) to avoid run-ins with vampires, gremlins, and werewolves, children must not go into the woods without an escort, especially at night; and (3) children must stay away from the lake, or they will be attacked by the kraken. The list of rules went on and on. After he was finished reciting them, Von Ulf handed everyone a schedule and a cabin assignment and bid the children goodnight.

Jason walked down the rows of cabins looking for the one he'd been assigned, #13. He tried hard not to stare at all the strange creatures that were lurking around. Ahead of him a moaning Zombie—with skin as white as snow and who was missing half of his face—limped down the path looking for his cabin. Next to him, a group of small, angry-looking goblins argued over a dead squirrel they had found on the ground. By the time Jason reached cabin

#13, his heart was thumping so loudly he thought it might jump out of his chest.

He stepped inside the cabin and closed the door behind him. He let out a great sigh of relief for making it there alive. Inside the small room there were two sets of bunk beds, a long wooden desk in the corner, a tiny bathroom, and a cramped closet. Jason plunked his bag down on the desk and felt a wave of panic pass over him as he noticed a body lying on one of the bottom bunk beds. But his panic quickly turned to relief when the person rolled over and he saw a familiar face.

"Miles!" he cried out. Jason ran over and sat down on the bed next to his friend. "Are you okay?"

"I've been better," said Miles shakily, propping himself up on his elbows. He looked rather pale, but alive.

Jason was overjoyed to find that he and Miles were going to be in the same cabin. But he wasn't happy when the door swung open and Chadwick Wellington XVII entered the room with his fancy suitcase and nose in the air. The hoity-toity boy stood in the doorway with perfect posture and a look on his face as if he smelled something rotten.

"This must be a sick joke," Chadwick said, looking around the room with disgust. He hauled his suitcase onto the desk, knocking Jason's to the floor. From his bag he pulled out a magnifying glass and handkerchief. Then he walked over to the opposite set of bunk beds. With the handkerchief he removed the sheets from the bottom bed and used the magnifying glass to inspect the mattress for bugs.

"I can't believe we're expected to live in these filthy conditions. I'm surprised that no one has contracted the plague by now!"

Jason soon found out why Chadwick acted like he was something special. He descended from a man named Chadwick Wellington III, who came to America on the *Mayflower* in 1620. During his trip across the sea, the boy's Pilgrim ancestor was pushed off the boat for arguing with another Pilgrim over a fish, but miraculously he survived by hanging on to the anchor until the boat reached Plymouth Rock. He later made a fortune by inventing the inner tube.

Many Chadwicks later, Chadwick Wellington XVI inherited much of the inner tube money; therefore, every summer, he sent his son away to some sort of camp to, as he put it, "get him out of his hair."

Jason and Miles watched as the boy dug into his suitcase, took out his own set of sheets and blankets, and began remaking the bed. As he turned his back towards them, Jason had to cover his mouth to keep from laughing out loud. Spelled out in mud on the back of the boy's pristine white jacket was the name BORIS.

"It could be a lot worse," said Jason, holding back his laughter.

The moment Jason had spoken, the door swung open again, and just like that, things got a lot worse. Standing in the doorway was their fourth roommate. He was about six feet tall and had a large skull with long wiry brown hair that hung to his shoulders, buck teeth, and one huge green eye smack in the middle of his forehead. He wore a T-shirt with a picture of a rock band called "Cronus" on it—the band consisted of four, one-eyed beasts like himself carrying guitars shaped like lightning bolts. He stood hunched over in the doorway, checking and rechecking that he had the correct cabin number, as if unable to believe his poor luck.

"Oh, great!" he said rolling his large eye. "I didn't think I'd have to share a room with a bunch of humans." When he spoke, flecks of spit flew from his mouth.

His name was Argophemus. He was a cyclops, and as they all quickly found out, he was very grumpy. Argophemus—like most cyclopes—lived in a cave and was stubborn, strong, and devoid of all emotion. His parents sent him to the retreat because he played his music too loudly, lost interest in his studies, and they thought he was falling in with the wrong crowd at school.

Argophemus and Chadwick quickly decided that they despised each other, and the bickering between them started almost immediately.

Argophemus climbed up the ladder to the top bunk above Chadwick. Then he flopped his head over the side of his bed and said, "You'd better not snore or talk in your sleep or anything. Don't touch any of my stuff, and don't bother me while I'm listening to my music."

"Don't worry. I'll pretend you don't exist. That weird eye of yours is really quite off-putting, your buck teeth are disgusting, and you spit all over the place when you talk," said Chadwick.

"*You're* really off-putting," Argophemus said. "How about I dump a pail full of spiders in your bed while you are asleep tonight and we'll see how *off-putting* that is to you!"

"If you do something like that, my father will sue you, you freak of nature!" Chadwick spat.

"Who are you calling a freak of nature, *two eyes*!" Argophemus yelled.

And on and on it went....

Once everyone was settled into the cabin and the lights were turned off, Jason had a hard time falling asleep. Argophemus and

Chadwick argued well into the night about everything, beginning with who had better eyesight and ending with a line of string being raised across two sticks, dividing up the room into halves. To make matters worse, Jason soon learned that Miles was the one who had a snoring problem.

The sound of wolves howling outside kept Jason on edge, and the wind whipping against his window caused him to shiver. For quite some time, he stared out the window overlooking the valley. He thought about Agnes and how she was probably laughing herself to sleep at the thought of having the house to herself all summer. Maybe she'd throw loud, raucous parties for all her evil nanny friends. Jason felt a surge of anger towards her for dumping him in this awful place.

Finally Jason managed to fall asleep, but soon after, he was awoken by a low scraping sound coming from the corner of the room. He jolted upright in bed, but it was too dark to see anything. The scraping noise continued, followed by a loud thump.

Jason peered over the side of his bed. As his eyes adjusted to the darkness, he saw a figure moving around near the desk in the corner of the room. It remained still for a moment, and then, to his horror, slowly began moving towards his bed. Jason held his breath. Someone, or *something,* was creaking up the ladder of his bunk! Then whoever, or *whatever,* it was, climbed onto Jason's bed.

In the puddle of moonlight coming through the window, Jason could see that a rather plump boy sat cross-legged at the foot of his bed. He had the palest skin that Jason had ever seen, and his jet-black hair was slicked back with a widow's peak framing his forehead. The boy's eyes were also black, and he had two long pointy front teeth that stuck out over his lower lip. It didn't take

Jason long to realize that the boy was a vampire and that the desk in the corner of the room wasn't a desk at all—it was a coffin!

Jason backed himself up against the wall, as far away as he could get from the vampire. He hugged his pillow to his chest, frozen with fear.

"Who put that stuff on my bed?" asked the boy. The tone of his voice was surprisingly soft. Jason saw that in his pale white hands he held a little brown ferret with beady eyes and whiskers. It had a long body and a white stripe down its back. The boy was petting it gently.

It took Jason a moment to answer. "We...uh...we thought it was a desk," he stuttered.

"It's not a desk, it's my bed," said the vampire calmly—in fact, a little more calmly than Jason would have expected a vampire to speak.

"I'm sorry," whispered Jason, his voice trembling. "I didn't know."

Jason had read a lot of books about vampires. He knew that they slept in coffins during the day, only came out at sundown, and liked to bite people and suck their blood. One bite from a vampire and you would live forever in a horrible state of half death. What was Von Ulf thinking putting him in the same room with such a dangerous creature?

As the boy sat silently staring at him, it began to occur to Jason that the vampire might not be very dangerous after all. He also wondered why the vampire was so plump. *Aren't vampires supposed to be gaunt and unhealthy looking?* he thought. This vampire looked like he rarely missed a meal!

"I'm not going to bite you, if that's what you're thinking," said the boy. "I don't like the taste of blood. I prefer vegetables and

chocolate." He patted his rather round belly.

"Really?" asked Jason. "But I thought vampires liked blood."

"We're supposed to, but I don't like it. It drives my parents crazy. That's why they sent me here," said the boy, shrugging his shoulders. "They feel that I'm 'not honoring vampiric traditions and culture.' I just think that vampires are unfairly stereotyped in society and feel unnecessary pressure to live up to their image. I believe a vampire should have the right to choose whether or not to live up to people's expectations."

"What's your name?" asked Jason.

The vampire sighed again and petted his ferret. "My name is Vlad, but I'm trying to legally change it. I hate it," he yawned. "It sounds so...vampirey."

"What do you want to change it to?" said Jason.

"I don't know." He puffed out his cheeks and exhaled. "I was thinking of maybe Steve or Dean. Those sound like good solid human names."

Jason loosened the grip he had on his covers. He seemed to be in no immediate peril. "Who's that?" Jason asked, pointing to the wriggling ferret that Vlad clutched in his hand.

"This is Miss Pinkerton. She's my pet ferret. My family tries to eat her all the time, so I had to take her with me." Vlad sighed. "It seems that you humans have it so much easier than us vampires do. You get to play in the sun, go swimming, and eat garlic. I've heard garlic is the tastiest thing around! I'd like to be a chef someday, but how can I be a chef if I can't go near garlic?"

"Yeah, garlic is okay," said Jason, "but I bet being a vampire could be pretty cool, too! You get to live forever and wear those cool capes!"

Vlad shrugged. "I guess. What's your name, anyway?"

"Jason Crawford."

"Well, it was good meeting you, Jason. I think I'll get going now. I have to work in the laundry room today. I only have about six more hours until I have to go back to bed!" Vlad sighed, as he began to climb down the ladder. "Thanks for talking to me. Being a vampire can be very lonely sometimes."

"Okay," said Jason. "Sorry about putting our stuff on your bed, Vlad. It won't happen again."

"No problem," said Vlad, "but call me Dean, okay?"

"Sure," agreed Jason.

"Good night, Jason!" The vampire shuffled lazily out of the cabin and closed the door behind him.

"Good night...Dean" said Jason. Trembling, Jason lay back down and pulled the covers over his head.

Chapter Six

Fairy Wings

The next morning Jason woke up to the sound of Argophemus and Chadwick arguing.

"This is my bed, and you aren't to touch it with any part of your body when you come down from your bed!" yelled Chadwick. "And I know it was you who threw my bag on the floor last night!"

"I didn't touch it!" Argophemus shouted back. "I wouldn't touch your bag or your filthy human bed for all the money in the world!"

"Your disgusting cyclopean blanket dropped down through the crack and brushed up against my arm in the middle of the night! Now I'm going to have to be quarantined!" Chadwick hollered, wiping his arm dramatically on the wall.

Jason peered down over his bunk at Miles. The color had come back into his face, but it carried the look of someone who didn't quite believe what was happening to him.

"How did you sleep?" Jason asked.

"As well as could be expected," Miles shrugged weakly.

Jason looked over at the coffin that, just yesterday, he'd assumed was a desk. He decided it might be a good time to tell everyone about the visitor he'd had last night.

"There's a vampire living in this room with us," he said.

"Don't you *dare* try to smother me in the middle of the night with your pillow or I...I...wait...*what?*" Chadwick stopped mid-sentence.

"Yeah...*what?*" quipped Miles, sitting up abruptly in his bed.

"Yep," Jason said, swinging his legs over the side of the bunk and pointing to the coffin. "His name is Vlad, but he wants to be called Dean. That's not a desk over there. That's his bed."

"You're crazy!" said Argophemus, slowly lowering the pillow he had raised above Chadwick's head. "They'd never pair us with a vampire. The nasty blood sucker would kill us all!"

"It's the truth," Jason said, jumping down from his bunk. "He woke me up last night and told me to keep my stuff off his bed."

"Whoa!" said Argophemus. "That's awesome!"

Chadwick looked pale. "What kind of sick joke is this, putting us in a room with a dangerous, blood sucking creature? As if this one-eyed freak isn't bad enough!" he said, pointing angrily at Argophemus.

"He doesn't like blood. He prefers vegetables," said Jason. "Actually, he was very nice."

"So he's in there? Right now?" Miles gulped and pointed to the coffin.

"Uh-huh!" said Jason. "He'll wake up sometime after the sun goes down."

Faced with the news of their nocturnal roommate, Argophemus and Chadwick put their verbal war on hold. All of a sudden everyone seemed very eager to get dressed and get out of the cabin.

Jason checked his schedule. He was to report to the kitchen for Mess Hall duty. As he stepped out of cabin #13, he inhaled a deep breath of the cool, early morning air and headed toward the kitchens. On the way, Jason looked out over the ridge of the mountain and saw for the first time how very scenic and beautiful the surroundings were. The fog that had hung over the lake had lifted and was replaced by an early morning mist. Down below, the valley was green and stretched for miles. The lake was sparkling blue, and the town itself looked tiny compared to the majestic mountain range surrounding it.

It was very early, and Jason was alone on the path. Fresh dew covered the grass, and the sound of chirping birds filled the air. *How bad could it be here?* he thought. It might be exciting to mingle with monsters, after all. He could learn a thing or two about them, and just wait until he told Oliver Jensen! He'd be so jealous! Jason caught himself smiling.

For a moment he felt peaceful and happy, and he almost laughed out loud at the thought of Agnes's plan to send him to a miserable place backfiring. But as Jason neared the Mess Hall, his peaceful thoughts came to an abrupt end. The sounds of angry shouting and the banging of pots and pans echoed from inside. Jason took a deep breath and pushed open the doors.

The kitchen was filled with sinks, ovens, and freezers. Bubbling pots simmered on the stoves. Smoke poured from the ovens. There were utensils hanging from wire racks and shelves lined with dishes. Boxes and bags of food were everywhere and several questionable smells wafted through the stuffy, hot air. Jason suppressed the urge to throw up.

"You're late!" a deep, manly voice called out to him. In the center of the room was a large and ugly woman. She was twice as big as any human he had ever seen...and twice as ugly. She had no teeth, a wart the size of a golfball on her whiskery chin, and two googly eyes that sat far apart on her lumpy face—each one looking in a different direction. She wore a stained apron and a hairnet, and was holding a wooden spoon that dripped with slimy gray goo. From the looks of her, Jason decided that she must be an ogre.

"I'm sorry. I got a little lost," Jason lied. He had actually just gotten a little caught up in his thoughts and had stared into the valley for too long. Jason's heart dropped when the ogre woman moved to the side and he saw Boris standing there, looking surprisingly tiny next to her. He sneered when he recognized Jason and buried one fist into another in a punching motion. Next to Boris stood a girl with at least 20 live hissing snakes sprouting from her head. Her arms were crossed and she sported a scowl on her face. Sitting on the floor against the refrigerator was Thelma Butterworth, and standing in the corner looking out the window was a big-footed boy completely covered with long, shaggy white hair.

The ogre waddled towards Jason and tossed a wrinkled apron at him. "My name is Helga, and I'm in charge of the kitchens here," she said in a gruff tone. "Today and every Monday for the rest of the summer, you will follow my instructions or get written up! At the end of the day I'll take your write-ups to Von Ulf and he'll record them in his Red Book. Trust me when I tell you, you don't want too many! Now...what's your name?"

"Jason Crawford."

Helga took a clipboard from her apron and scanned it with her bubble-eyes. "Ahh...Mr. Imagination, eh?" she said sarcastically. Then she added sternly, "Playtime's over. Welcome to reality! Put on that apron, grab a spoon, and get busy stirring that stew I started!" She pointed to a large black kettle that was bubbling on a nearby stove.

Jason reluctantly went over to the pot. It had large brown chunks of the foulest meat he'd ever smelled. With one hand he plugged his nose, and with the other he slowly began stirring the thick slop. It was like trying to mix cement.

"There are many different species here at the retreat, and I'm responsible for feeding all of them and their various appetites!"

Helga explained loudly to the group.

"What about my appetite?" Thelma blurted out. "I'm starving!"

"Get up and earn your breakfast! There are no hand-outs here!" Helga said. "Laziness will not go unpunished!"

Thelma rolled her eyes and lifted herself off the ground with great effort.

"Gorgonia," Helga said to the girl with snakes coming out of her head, "you'll work with Mr. Imagination today. You two will be in charge of feeding the trolls, ogres, goblins, and giants. I suggest you get the recipes correct—these aren't the type who take lightly to hunger!"

"Boris and Thelma, you two are in charge of land dwellers, humans, and bloodsuckers. And Yeti," she said, pointing to the white-furred boy by the window, "you'll work with me today feeding the water, air, and swamp dwellers."

Yeti sighed and slowly shuffled over to Helga, almost tripping over his own large feet.

"The recipes you're responsible for today are on the counter," Helga yelled. "Now let's get moving everyone, we've got a lot of mouths to feed this summer!"

Gorgonia walked over to Jason. Aside from her snake-infested head and fiery red eyes, she looked like a human, but she moved like a reptile. Jason was immediately terrified of her.

"Give me that *ssss*patula," she hissed, "and quit *sss*taring at my head, human!"

Jason carefully passed the spatula to her. She ripped it from his hands and bared her teeth, which were sharp and pointy. A low, guttural-sounding noise came from her throat as the snakes on her head writhed and hissed. They were thin and black, and had fiery red eyes that matched hers.

Jason looked at the recipes, and for the second time that morning, he almost threw up.

FROG BISCUITS:

Combine four dozen minced swamp frogs and a pinch of tortoise brain

Mix three dozen eggs with 5 pints of mud

Sprinkle with breadcrumbs

Bake in the oven for 45 minutes at 350°; then serve

FAUN STEW:

Stir together 10 lbs of faun meat with 2 lbs of bat blood

Add the hair of a gnome

Mix 1 cup of fresh grated fairy wings into stew

Garnish with a rabbit's foot; then serve

Feeling queasy, Jason looked at the ingredients provided to their cooking station. The awful-smelling chunks that were already bubbling in the pots were the faun meat. There was a disgusting bowl of minced green stuff that Jason figured were tortoise brains and swamp frogs. A jar of hair labeled GNOME and a bottle of red liquid labeled *Farmer Forlord's Delicious Bat Blood™* sat on the counter. But Jason gasped when he saw what was just behind the blood. Sitting at the back of the counter was a glass jar holding three, very live fairies. They were the most beautiful creatures Jason had ever seen. They fluttered around in circles, wearing dresses made from leaves. They had silky gossamer wings and long hair that shimmered in the light. The fairies looked very frightened and quite agitated as they bumped into each other and up against the sides of the glass. In their desperation, they were releasing little bursts of silver glitter.

"Excuse me, Helga?" said Jason.

"What?" she croaked. Helga was in the middle of yelling at Boris for sticking a scorpion he'd found in the freezer down the back of Thelma's shirt.

"The recipe says that we have to pull the wings off of these fairies. But that would kill them, wouldn't it?" Jason asked.

"Of course it would. Fairy wings are a delicacy," she said, licking her lips. "They wouldn't taste the same unless they were fresh!"

Jason's heart sunk. "But they are so...beautiful!" he said. He couldn't imagine killing the fairies.

Helga snorted. "Silly boy, fairies are common pests. They're as bad as houseflies are to you humans. Now get to work! Breakfast is served in an hour."

Jason found that working with Gorgonia wasn't fun. She was very bossy and the snakes on her head nipped at his hands if he got in her way or didn't move fast enough. The smells from the Faun Stew and the Frog Biscuits, combined with the heat from the ovens, were making him nauseous. Plus, he was dreading the point in the recipe when they would have to add fairy wings into the stew.

Helga's loud screams filled the air, causing Jason's head to ache on top of everything else. To add to the noise, Yeti was wailing because Boris had tied his fur to a chair, causing him to trip and chip a snaggletooth. Soon Jason's head was pounding, and he was dripping with sweat. It was then that he heard the strange beeping sound he had first heard in the tunnel the night before. It seemed to be coming from somewhere near the fairy jar, but he couldn't be sure.

"Do you hear that?" he asked Gorgonia.

"Hear *what*?" she hissed. "Quit *sss*talling and hand me that bottle of gnome hair!"

Just then there was a loud crash. Thelma had been reaching for something on the top shelf and accidently spilled a jar filled with tarantulas—used in the recipe for Zombie Pot Pie. There was broken glass on the floor, and large hairy spiders scrambling all over.

"I don't feel like doing this. When can we have a TV break?" Thelma whined.

"Stop being so lazy or else I'll have to tell Mr. Von Ulf!" Helga snapped.

"I don't care!" yelled Thelma, crossing her arms over her belly and stomping her foot. "I'm bored, and I don't want to do this anymore!"

"Look what you've done!" Helga yelled. "Get a broom and sweep up those tarantulas!"

Jason wiped the sweat from his brow and leaned his elbows on the counter, trying to block everything out—the horrid smells, the annoying beeping sound, and the yelling. He tried to ignore Gorgonia's demands. "Keep *sss*stirring the *sss*tew, *sss*illy human!" she insisted. Jason put his face down and focused on the fairies. One of them flew up the side of the jar, her big blue eyes filled with worry.

"Can you hear me?" she said in a tiny voice. Suddenly it was as if that was all he could hear. All the other sounds in the room faded away into the background.

"Yes, I can hear you," Jason said. Surprised, he glanced around to see if anyone was paying attention. Amid the chaos, nobody was.

"What's your name?" asked the fairy.

"It's Jason Crawford. What's yours?"

"My name is Wilhelmina," she said, smiling. "How old are you?"

"Ten."

"Do you know why you're here?"

"Because an evil woman named Agnes sent me here," Jason replied.

She turned to the other fairies and shook her head sadly. "He doesn't know."

A second fairy came up to the side of the jar and peered at Jason with curiosity. She had long red hair and green eyes.

"Will he be okay?" the second fairy asked Wilhelmina.

Jason didn't know what the fairies were talking about. "What do you mean, *will he be okay*?" he demanded.

"He's in danger," said the first fairy to the second.

"You're the ones who are in danger," whispered Jason.

Wilhelmina giggled. "Why is that?" she asked sweetly.

"Because Helga wants me to kill you, and I don't want to," said Jason.

"What is he saying?" asked the third fairy. "He's not making sense." She came up to the side of the glass to join the others. She was scowling and not as pretty as the other two fairies.

Poor things, Jason thought. They didn't even know what was about to happen to them.

"I don't want to tear your wings off, but I'll get in trouble if I don't," he said.

"Who does he want to kill?" asked the second fairy.

"Probably me," said the third fairy, crossing her arms and

pouting.

"I don't know what you're all talking about," said Jason, secretly thinking that fairies were weird, "but you're about to be killed and made into Faun Stew. If I let you go, will you fly away?"

"Faun Stew? What an imagination!" The red-haired fairy laughed.

"At least he's talking to us. That's a good sign," the second fairy said. "Usually they don't at this point."

"What point?" Jason asked. Just then a dark shadow fell over the jar and he heard a booming voice above him.

"Excuse me!" It was Helga, and she was standing over him with her hands on her hips. "Whom are you talking to?"

Startled, Jason jumped. "The fairies," he said, pointing to the jar. "They started to talk to me."

"What an imagination!" said Helga. "Fairies can't talk!"

"But they were! They were just talking to me!" cried Jason. He looked back at the jar. Inside, all three were circling around the jar again, acting like regular old fairies.

"Right, and I'm the Queen of Fog Valley!" Helga spat. "Quit daydreaming and get to work. Those wings are almost ready to come off!" She stormed away.

In no time at all, the recipe was almost complete. Gorgonia had taken the Frog Biscuits out of the oven, and the Faun Stew was simmering. They had set the tables in the Mess Hall, and in only ten minutes, the rest of the camp would be coming in for breakfast. All that was left were the final touches and then breakfast would be ready.

Jason stalled for time by pretending to look for a stray tarantula that had escaped underneath the cupboard. He hoped that Helga wouldn't notice that the fairy wings weren't in the stew. He felt someone coming up behind him and cringed when he heard Boris's voice.

"Where's my money for today, nerd?"

"I told you, I'm not paying you," Jason said, standing to face him.

"Do you want another punch in the nose?" asked Boris. "I'd figured you'd had enough already."

"Why don't you pick on someone your own size...like Helga?" Jason said. "I bet you wouldn't be so tough then!"

"I'm not afraid of that ogre", Boris scoffed.

"You'll get written up by Von Ulf," Jason pointed out.

"I don't care," said Boris. "I'm not afraid of that old lunatic either!"

"Just leave me alone, Boris," said Jason.

"Crazy freak," Boris scoffed, "talking to a bunch of fairies! Maybe I'll just take them and kill them myself." He started reaching for the jar.

Jason threw down the spoon he was holding and blocked the jar. "Don't," he said, "or else..."

"Or else what?" asked Boris, grinning maliciously.

"Just don't." Jason took the jar in his hands and held it to his chest. The fairies were excited. They fluttered around nervously, their wings beating against the jar.

"Give me those fairies!" Boris yelled. He lunged for the jar, but Jason was too quick; he ducked and ran to the other end of the stove. Without even thinking, Jason unscrewed the top of the lid and watched as all three fairies circled up and flew out of the jar.

From across the room Helga saw what was happening and cried out, "NOOOOOOOO!"

In an instant the fairies made a beeline to the top shelves, where their three tiny wands had been hidden. From there they flew above the room, pointed their wands, and sprinkled green dust, causing everyone, including Jason, to break out into an itchy rash and a fit of violent sneezing. Then, with everyone preoccupied, the fairies circled above Helga, joined hands, and then FLASH! A bright light momentarily lit up the room. Finally the fairies flew out the window, leaving everyone stunned—everyone except for Helga, who was no longer there. In her place was a giant hippopotamus with long whiskers and a wart the size of a golf ball on its chin.

After the pandemonium in the kitchens had broken out, the dwarfs were called in to secure the situation. Helga the Hippo had gone on a tirade. She had stomped around the kitchens, tipping over tables and breaking things, until she eventually crashed through the window and escaped into the woods. Boris and Gorgonia got into a verbal fight, which turned into a food fight, and then turned into a dish fight. It was Boris vs. Gorgonia (plus all of the snakes on her head) throwing plates, spoons, forks, knives, glasses, and whatever else they could launch at each other from across the kitchen. Thelma Butterworth sprained her ankle trying to run for cover, and Yeti was found hanging from a ceiling fan by his fur. The kitchen was left in shambles.

Since he had started the ruckus by freeing the fairies, Jason had been escorted directly to Von Ulf's office. It was there that he now sat. All around him were shelves filled with books and journals. Papers and file folders were strewn across the desk and framed articles about the retreat covered the walls.

The door opened and Von Ulf limped in on his cane. He took a seat behind his long desk and pulled out a large red book from the top drawer. Then he cleared his throat.

Uh-oh, thought Jason. There it was—the dreaded Red Book that Helga had mentioned.

"Well, well, Mr. Crawford," Von Ulf began, scratching his chin and looking down at a folder with Jason's name on it. "Would you please explain what happened today in the kitchen?"

"It was Boris Stubbs's fault," Jason said. "He's been harassing me since I got on the bus to come here."

"Don't worry about him. He's been written up in the Red Book as well...twice already," said Von Ulf. "Right now we're talking about you and the consequences of your actions." He raised his scarred eyebrow.

Jason looked down.

"Now, tell me what happened with the fairies," Von Ulf said.

"Boris was going to kill the fairies! I had to let them go!"

"The recipe called for fairy wings," Von Ulf said bluntly. "That is what goblins, ogres, and trolls consider nourishment," he added. "You know that one of the things we teach you here is to respect others' differences and to accept things that may not be what you are used to. That's an essential part of being a responsible person."

"Yes...but, I just couldn't!" cried Jason. "They were just so... beautiful."

"Setting those fairies free allowed them to cast a horrible spell on Helga. We found her grazing in the reeds near the lake," said Von Ulf. "Thank goodness there was a way to reverse the charm."

"I'm sorry about Helga," Jason said. "I didn't know the fairies would cast a spell."

Von Ulf scribbled something in his file. "Now Helga informed me that right before you freed the fairies, you were talking to them?"

"I was," Jason said quietly.

"Why?" asked Von Ulf.

"They were talking to me, so I answered them," Jason replied.

Von Ulf stared at him for a moment with unsettling black eyes. "I see that one of the reasons your nanny sent you here was because she feels you have an overactive imagination," he said.

"That's her opinion." Hearing about Agnes made him feel even worse. "And she's not my nanny," he mumbled.

"Fairies don't talk," Von Ulf stated firmly, putting the file in a drawer and slamming it shut. "And what happened today is a perfect example of how an overactive imagination can harm others. That kind of behavior will not be tolerated here." He took a pen from his desk and marked a big X in the Red Book.

"What's that?" asked Jason.

"You have an official write-up. You don't want too many of these," Von Ulf warned, pointing at the large X.

"What happens then?" asked Jason.

"Let's hope you don't find out. That's all for now," he said, and waved Jason out of the room with a flick of his hand.

"It isn't fair. Boris was going to kill the fairies, so I had to do something," Jason told Miles later that night at their cabin. "It wasn't my fault they cast a spell on Helga. Maybe if she wasn't trying to eat them, they wouldn't have!"

Miles nodded. "Well, if it makes you feel any better, I had a miserable day in the garden. A family of gnomes buried me up to my neck in the dirt because I had accidentally planted some Venus Flytraps over their house. How was I supposed to know? And another thing—those aren't horses in the stables. They're centaurs, and they are mean! One escaped from the stables today and almost ripped my arm off!"

"I just don't understand how no one else heard the fairies talking," said Jason, preoccupied with his own problems. "I know that sometimes I have a wild imagination, but this was different. I heard them!"

"What were they saying?" asked Miles.

Jason shrugged. The truth was, he didn't know where to begin. The fairies had been talking, but they hadn't been making much sense. They had said he was in danger, but Jason just figured they were confused. Why would he be in danger? It also occurred to him that the beeping noise he'd heard was probably made by a sneaky fairy and was created to get his attention. It was all probably an elaborate scheme to make him feel sorry for them and release them.

Argophemus was lying on his bunk listening to his headphones, and Chadwick was sitting at Dean's coffin, still treating it as if it were a desk. He refused to believe that a vampire lived in the room with them and was writing a long detailed letter of complaint to his father's lawyer after his harrowing day in the centaur stables. Apparently Chadwick was surprised and disgusted when he learned that centaurs had the lower body of a horse and the upper body of a human—and had nasty tempers. When he was instructed to brush them and polish their shoes, he refused. Instead, he began a long speech about how filthy and unsavory the centaurs smelled, and how they were probably carrying ticks and mites in their fur. Chadwick was quite offended when one of the centaurs kicked him straight into the mud and then escaped into the garden.

Afterwards another centaur stuffed hay into Chadwick's mouth and yelled at him for an hour.

"Hopefully tomorrow will be a better day," sighed Miles.

"It has to be," said Jason.

Jason awoke with a start in the middle of the night. Something warm and soft was tickling his face. It was Miss Pinkerton, Dean's pet ferret.

"Sorry!" whispered Dean. He was kneeling above Jason. "Miss Pinkerton escaped when I got out of bed, and she climbed up to see you. Sorry to wake you."

"That's okay," said Jason. "I wasn't sleeping very well anyway."

Even though Dean had told Jason he didn't like blood, it just didn't feel right waking up in the middle of the night with a vampire leaning over him.

"Did you have a good day?" asked Dean.

"No," Jason answered. He told Dean about his day in the kitchen with Helga, letting loose the fairies, and his trip to Von Ulf's office. "Fairies talk, don't they Dean?" he asked.

Dean paused. "Well, I've never know them to, but if you say the fairies were talking to you, I believe you."

"Thanks," said Jason. "It wasn't my imagination. I really heard them." Jason was frustrated. Everyone he spoke to insisted that fairies didn't talk. He was beginning to think he might be losing his mind after all.

"I'm sorry to hear you had a bad day," Dean said.

"You know, you're pretty nice for a..." Jason stopped himself midsentence. "Sorry."

"That's okay," said Dean, "you can say it—a vampire. I feel like you're my only friend here. There are no other vampires, so I have no one to hang out with at night. Werewolves only come out when there's a full moon, and they aren't very friendly, as you can imagine. I have to do my lessons and chores alone with the night staff, and so far they're a very crabby bunch."

"Well, I hope your night is better than my day was," said Jason.

Dean took Miss Pinkerton and began climbing down from the bunk. "Oh, one more thing," he whispered. "I don't think you want to get written up too many more times."

"Why? What happens then?"

"I've lived in Fog Valley all my life, and let's just say, things aren't always what they seem," Dean explained.

"What do you mean?" asked Jason.

"Well, for one thing, don't ever cross Von Ulf on nights when there's a full moon."

"Why?"

"Let's just say there's no telling what he might do," said Dean, and with that, he shuffled to the floor and out of the cabin.

Jason looked out the window at the moon. It was only a sliver in the sky, but he shuddered to think that soon it would be full.

Chapter Seven

The Blue Pixie

"Thelma Butterworth, you better get off that rock, pick up that shovel, and start digging!" Bonestraggler, one of the discipline leaders at Von Ulf's Retreat, was standing on a tree stump shouting into a megaphone. He was Jason's least favorite adult in Fog Valley—that is, if one can consider a goblin to be an "adult."

Jason had been at the retreat for exactly three weeks now. He had survived talking fairies in the Mess Hall with Helga, counseling on Thursdays with a moody witch named Miss Harklestorm, and daily bouts of harassment by the likes of Boris and Fern. But the one thing he dreaded the most were Fridays with Bonestraggler. The goblin was about three feet tall and had the shriveled up features of a prune. He was mean and spiteful. He'd pinch the children if they didn't do exactly as he said, and he always threatened to take them into the woods and cook them into a stew if they didn't listen. Jason wasn't sure if this was just a way of scaring them into behaving, but he was sure he didn't want to find out.

Friday at *Von Ulf's* was called Outdoor Day, and the day included activities around the campgrounds or challenges in the woods and lake. Each activity was a lesson concerning discipline, respect, and manners.

During the first Outdoor Day, Jason and the others in his group had to walk blindfolded over a small plank above a pit where a fire-breathing dragon lived, while Bonestraggler shouted out directions—a lesson in trust and discipline. The following week Jason and his group participated in a dangerous activity in the lake that promoted cooperation and communication. The children had been divided into teams and were instructed to work with one another and the lake dwellers to find a way through an underwater maze wearing scuba gear. Jason ended up tangled in a clump of seaweed while being poked by angry seahorses as the Kraken steadily approached. He narrowly escaped thanks to the help of a friendly mermaid named Greta. She had emerged from behind a rock, confessed her love of humans, and ferried Jason to the surface just in time. Then Greta had given Jason an awkward "high five" and a "thumbs-up" before diving back beneath the surface, leaving him choking and gasping for air on the shore.

"Tonight's challenge will concern the important virtues of respect and cooperation," growled Bonestraggler.

Tonight? Jason thought. Usually they had challenges during the daytime. All day they had been building new stables for the centaurs. Earlier that week the stables had caught fire, and rumor had it that Von Ulf knew who caused the blaze. The building had completely burned down, sending the centaurs on a wild stampede around the campgrounds. They ate all the carrots from the garden, kicked up the freshly planted Venus Flytraps, and ended up gathered around Cabin #13 holding torches, shouting for Chadwick Wellington XVII to "Come out and show his spoiled, rotten human face." Apparently they still hadn't forgiven him for calling them filthy, flea-ridden beasts.

"But tonight is a full moon!" yelled Fern Pratt.

Fern hadn't been doing too well at the retreat. Jason quickly learned that not only was she a thief, but a compulsive liar, too. On her second day at the retreat, Von Ulf caught her sneaking out of her cabin at night to look for fairies. Oddly enough at the time, he told her to find a rock from the forest and to start a pile just outside the campground. Every time she was caught lying or stealing, she was told to add a another rock to the pile. Three weeks later, the pile had grown so tall that it took her 15 minutes just to climb to the top to add another rock.

Jason couldn't stand Fern. He still hadn't forgotten how she'd stolen Miles's money on the bus, or more recently, how she'd found out that a vampire was sleeping in their room. Soon afterward she tried to pry open Vlad's coffin with a metal stake to see if he would shrivel up in the sunlight. Luckily one of the dwarfs caught her before she did any harm. And of course the dwarf had her add more rocks to her pile.

"You'll be divided into teams of two and sent into the woods," Bonestraggler explained. "You'll have to work with your partner and the inhabitants of the forest in order to reach your goal. There is a coin with your name on it hidden somewhere in the woods. Follow the clues to find it."

Chadwick raised his hand and stepped forward. "Excuse me, Mr. Bonespackler, or whatever your name is. I don't think it is responsible for this establishment to send us into those woods on the night of a full moon when there are bloodsucking creatures lurking about. My father won't be happy."

The goblin pinched Chadwick's arm roughly and shoved him back into line. "Only when you have your coin can you exit the forest," he continued. "Those who return without a coin will get written up. Remember that gremlins, trolls, and vampires will be lurking about. And they will be more than happy to eat you for dinner. Teamwork and honor is of the essence. Respect the creatures who live in the woods, and they will help you. Disrespect them, and they won't."

Jason was dismayed when he found out he was paired with Fern Pratt. Miles's partner was Elgor, a swamp dweller who was draped in green seaweed and smelled like mold. Argophemus was partnered with Yolanda Jones, Thelma was paired with Yeti, Boris and Gorgonia were another team, and a witch named Astrid was partnered with Robby Bowman, the boy who would eat nothing but candy and whose teeth had since fallen out because of it. Finally, Chadwick was partnered with a mummy named...well, nobody knew his name because he was wrapped from head to toe in rags and mostly just moaned and bumped into things.

"Oh, and one more thing," Bonestraggler growled. "You'll be chained to your partner, so cooperation is required."

Great, thought Jason, looking over at Fern, who stuck her tongue out at him.

Bonestraggler chained the teammates together by their wrists, leaving only three feet of space between them, and handed each of the teams a lantern and their first clue.

Fern read their clue aloud. "The tallest in the woods, I'm dressed in green. Follow the shimmering stones; it's easier than it seems."

"Dressed in green...it's got to be a tree," said Jason. "The tallest one in the woods."

"Obviously, genius," Fern said sarcastically, tugging the chain so hard that Jason almost lost his balance.

Bonestraggler blew a whistle, and the pairs set off into the forest. Jason had a very uneasy feeling. He'd never been in the woods at night, and he wasn't particularly excited to be going now, when there was a full moon. In the distance, he heard the howling of werewolves and oddly enough, the strange beeping noise again. It seemed to be coming from somewhere deep within the woods.

"Do you hear that, Fern?" Jason asked.

"Hear what?"

"That beep," said Jason.

"Sure I do," Fern replied with a shrug.

Finally! Someone else heard it! Jason thought. Although, he didn't know if he actually believed Fern, since almost everything that came out of her mouth was a lie.

As they ventured into the darkness, Jason saw a trail of bright silver stones on the path ahead. In the light of the full moon, the stones shimmered and sparkled.

"These are the stones we need to follow," Jason said.

Fern was walking impatiently in front of him. She was looking around, not quite paying attention and rudely kicking the stones and pulling the leaves off of the trees and the bushes as she walked by. She seemed very distracted and bored, as if she was looking for trouble.

"This is boring," Fern complained. "Let's go explore—in there!" She pointed to the thick trees.

"No," said Jason, tugging on the chain attached to her wrist.

"I want to find the Blue Pixie," she whined.

"What's the Blue Pixie?"

"You've never heard of the Blue Pixie?" Fern said incredulously. "She's a very rare pixie, and if you catch her, you get three wishes granted."

"I've never heard of anything like that. It doesn't sound possible," said Jason, although, he had been in Fog Valley long enough to know that anything was possible.

"My roommate, Astrid, told me all about it. She's a witch, and she knows things about the forest because she grew up here," said Fern, with her nose in the air. "It's more important to find the Blue Pixie than any stupid coin."

"Well, the directions were to find the coin, not some pixie," remarked Jason. "I can't get written up again in the Red Book. Let's just get this over with."

"Chicken," teased Fern, rudely spitting out the gum she was chewing and hitting a passing elf in the head.

"Fern! You're supposed to respect the forest!" Jason yelled. Already she had stomped on a clump of mushrooms, ripped out a handful of wildflowers, and thrown a rock at a fairy's tree house, breaking its window.

They continued down the path where the trees around them seemed to thicken, blocking out the moon and making it very difficult to see. The voices of the other pairs of children became faint as they headed off after their own clues, and soon they were completely alone. Jason clutched their lantern and concentrated on following the shimmering stones while trying to keep Fern's attention. Suddenly a fork in the path appeared. The stones went down both ways.

"Uh-oh," said Jason. "Which one do we follow?"

"How do I know?" asked Fern. "I say we ditch this game and go explore the cyclops caves. I heard that..."

"Shhh!" Jason interrupted her, turning abruptly towards the edge of the trees behind them. He had heard a rustling noise. Jason froze when he saw something move.

"It's a moving tree!" Fern exclaimed. She went over to the tree, picked up a large stick, and poked the tree with it.

"OOOOOOOWWWWWCCH!" A voice from above boomed down at them.

Fern screamed and jumped behind Jason. Suddenly they heard the sound of branches cracking, and it felt like the forest was collapsing. Three trees bent down, and Jason was astonished to find that they weren't trees at all, but the legs of three giants!

The giants towered over them and stared down with their huge blue eyes. They were about 25 feet tall with hands like boulders, and even though they had bent down, they were still high above Jason and Fern.

"What are you two doing in the woods tonight?" asked the giant whom Fern had poked with the stick. He wore a felt hat and a rope around his neck with some kind of animal bone for a charm. He was a few feet taller than the other two, and his loud voice echoed, sending the birds flying from the trees.

Jason was scared. "We...we are staying at Von Ulf's Retreat," he managed. "We're on a hunt to find a coin."

"Wow! You are *huge*!" said Fern, slowly moving from behind Jason. "Can I sit on your head and see how far I can see over the treetops?"

The giant ignored her and focused on Jason. "The woods are very dangerous," he said. "I know many creatures who would pay a lot of gold to have two human children for dinner."

Jason shuddered. "Please, sir. We're just here to find a coin and then we'll be gone."

"What kind of bone is that?" Fern asked. She was staring at the giant's necklace.

"This is the bone of a human girl WHO WAS VERY RUDE AND POKED GIANTS WITH STICKS IN THE FOREST!" answered the angry giant in a booming voice.

This quieted Fern immediately.

"We've been told to find the tallest in the forest. Would that be you?" asked Jason, noticing the green shirt the giant wore.

The giant nodded. "It is I."

"Do you have a clue for us?" asked Jason.

"We do," replied the giant.

"How'd you guys get to be so big?" Fern rudely interrupted.

The giant raised his eyebrow and scowled.

"Excuse me," said Jason, as he nudged Fern. "Don't mind her. Please can we have the next clue?"

"What brings you to Von Ulf's Retreat?" asked one of the giants.

"Well, supposedly I have an overactive imagination," explained Jason. "I'm trying to work on it, but Fog Valley is actually not the best place for that!"

Fern, who obviously was no longer afraid, stepped forward and pointed at the giants. "My father is Mr. Von Ulf!" she lied. "He's made me in charge for the summer!"

"Lying is a bad sign," said the tallest giant, shaking his head.

Great, thought Jason. Now that he was with Fern the liar, automatically he was going to be accused of fibbing as well.

"I'm not lying, I swear. That's why I'm here!" Fern continued to lie. "My father, Mr. Von Ulf, wanted you to put me on your head and give me a lift back to the cabins. He'll pay you in gold!"

"*I'm* telling you the truth," said Jason, beating on his chest with his fist. "I have no reason to lie."

"Tsk, tsk," said one of the giants to the others. "Obviously their problems aren't improving. Talking nonsense is not a good sign. At this rate, neither of them will ever leave here."

"Whatever!" Fern yelled. "You giants bore me. Where are the gremlins?"

"Fern!" Jason scolded, turning to look her straight in the eye. "Stop it!"

"Stop what?" she asked. Her nostrils were flaring in the same way Agnes's did when she was unhappy. "These giants aren't listening to me!" She stomped her foot on the ground.

"Fern!" Jason yelled again. "She didn't mean to be rude, sir.

She's just scared," he lied.

All of a sudden, with just two fingers, the tallest giant picked Fern up by the back of her shirt. She screamed as he lifted her up to his eye and stared at her. Since Jason was chained to her wrist, he had no choice but to be lifted off the ground, too. Now they were both dangling 25 feet in the air.

"Do you know how easy it would be for me to sell you to the trolls for gold?" the giant asked, ignoring Fern's screams.

Jason hung there, swinging back and forth, as the giant reprimanded Fern. He felt as if his stomach had dropped. He looked down at the ground, which seemed so very far away, and prayed that the giant would take mercy on them. But instead the oversized creature just bellowed and tossed the pair of children to another giant, as if they were a football. Back and forth, back and forth, they were passed until Jason felt dizzy and sick.

"Please!" he yelled. "Just let us down!"

"Let you down?" asked the giant. "Have it your way!" He placed the two of them in the highest branch of a tree and, with that, he and the others left.

Jason and Fern clung to the tree branch until the booming of the giants' footsteps faded in the distance. Then slowly they began climbing down from the tree. After carefully maneuvering around branches and the chain—and many cuts and scrapes later—they made it to the bottom. Now they were alone, stuck in the middle of the forest on the night of a full moon, without a clue as to how to reach the coin. Things didn't look good.

"Great, Fern!" Jason said angrily, brushing leaves from his shirt. "Those giants were our only hope of getting a clue!"

"Who needs them anyway?" said Fern stubbornly.

"We do! Now which way do we go?" Jason asked. Panic was

beginning to settle in his bones. Both paths looked exactly the same—scary and dark and lined with black, overhanging trees and twisting branches. Jason thought for a moment, realizing he had to make a choice. He picked up the lantern, took a deep breath, and started walking down the path on the left. He hoped he'd made the right decision. Fern followed reluctantly behind him. The woods were alive with strange noises. Howling wolves, croaking frogs, and ghastly shrieks echoed in the night air. Jason was terrified.

"Wait! I just saw something!" Fern said, stopping suddenly. She peered into the trees away from the path.

"You didn't, Fern," said Jason, bored. "We need to find the coin. Those giants almost sold us to trolls. Stay focused, will you?"

"Look over there!" Fern pointed into the darkness. "I really saw something. It was blue and glowing. I think it was the Blue Pixie!"

"Fern, if this is another one of your lies..." Jason warned. Something told him that he shouldn't go with her, but at this point he didn't know what else to do. If she was right about the Blue Pixie, then that was exactly what they might need to get out of the forest in one piece.

"Follow me!" Fern tugged Jason off the path and dragged him through the thick foliage. Soon they reached a clearing where a crumbling stone well stood.

Why is this well sitting in the middle of nowhere? Jason wondered. Something didn't seem right.

"I saw her go down the well," Fern said excitedly.

"I don't believe you, Fern," said Jason.

"I saw her!" Fern's eyes were wild, a mix of fear and excitement. "It could be our only chance. If we catch the Blue Pixie, we can make a wish to get out of here!"

"Well, how do we go after her?" Jason asked, looking around nervously.

Fern was leaning over the side of the deep well. "Look! There's a ladder!" she exclaimed. "Come and see for yourself!"

"I don't think it's a good idea," Jason said.

"C'mon. *Baby*!" Fern teased. "Just take a peek."

Jason reluctantly walked to the well and leaned over the side. He squinted his eyes, but couldn't see a thing except for the deep, dark abyss. He was about to turn around and drag Fern straight back onto the path, but just then he heard something at the bottom of the well.

"Come with us..." the voice whispered. *"We've been waiting for you...."*

It sounded menacing and sinister, causing a chill to go down Jason's spine. Suddenly the words of the fairies from Helga's kithcen echoed in his memory. *He's in danger...* they had said.

"Fern, did you hear that?" Jason asked, and just then he felt two hands pressing against his back. He suddenly lost his balance and his grip on the lantern, and toppled over the side of the well. At the last moment, he managed to clutch onto the rim with one hand. Hanging over the abyss, he looked down and watched as the lantern tumbled down, lighting up the dark hole. What Jason saw made him scream. Huddled at the bottom of the well were several yellow-eyed gremlins staring up at him. They were furry with long pointed ears, sharp teeth, and claws. As they caught sight of Jason in the light, they started screeching all at once. It was an awful wail. Then, as he held onto the rim for dear life, Jason heard the gremlins slowly climbing up the sides walls.

After she'd pushed him, Fern covered her mouth with her free hand and giggled wickedly above him. But when the lantern cast its light on the gremlins, she started screaming in fear and tried to pull Jason back up with the chain still attached to her wrist. But she wasn't strong enough, and once she realized this, she reached for a large rock with her free hand and desperately began striking the chain with it, attempting to detach herself from Jason and the approaching gremlins.

"Don't let go, Fern! Help me!" Jason called out desperately. He was afraid to look down, but he could hear the gremlins cackling as they crawled up the sides of the well to claim him as dinner. These sounds were mixed with the banging of stone on metal from above.

"It's time to go," hissed the gremlins. "Come with us...."

"Fern! Help me!" he yelled. Jason could feel his grip loosening on the damp rim of the well. Then he heard a heavy thud and felt Fern break free from the chain. She ran away, leaving him barely hanging on.

"Fern! Come back!" Jason cried. Terrified, he looked down and saw the long bony arm of a gremlin reaching for his ankle. He tried again to get a foothold on the side of the well, but his feet slipped against the wet, slimy stone.

"Come with usssss..." the gremlins continued to hiss, with their yellow eyes glowing and their sharp teeth bared.

Jason could feel himself slipping...slipping...slipping....

"I don't want to die! Help!" he cried with all the strength he could muster. His arms were trembling.

Suddenly he heard voices above him.

"Help!" Jason hollered again. He looked up, and he could see two figures leaning over the side of the well. They each grabbed hold of the chain that was still attached to Jason's wrist and pulled.

"Come on, Jason! Hang on!" one of them yelled. "We've got you!"

Jason could feel the hands of several gremlins clutching his pant leg and tugging forcefully.

"One...two...three..." the figure above counted out, "PULL!"

All at once, Jason felt the gremlins release their grip as he tumbled out of the well and into the mud.

"Are you okay?" asked Miles. He and Elgor had used their combined strength to pull Jason to safety.

"Yes," Jason panted.

"It was lucky that we found you!" remarked Elgor.

"Where did you come from?" Jason asked.

"We got lost near the caves after we found our coin. Then a werewolf chased us—I think it was Mordico. Argophemus and Yolanda...I think..." Miles gulped.

"What?"

"I think Mordico caught them. I'm not sure...." He looked down. "Then I heard you screaming, so we had to come help."

"You saved my life. Thank you, both of you," said Jason, slowly raising himself out of the mud.

Exhausted, the three somehow found their way out of the woods. Back at the camp, they were happy to see that Argophemus was all right. He had a few scratches on his face from tangling with Mordico, who had been on a full-moon werewolf rampage. The only reason that Argophemus escaped was that his partner, Yolanda Jones, had cleverly used the lantern to set a fire that distracted the werewolf.

Chadwick sat sulking on a tree stump, still attached to the mummy, who was twiddling his thumbs and moaning about something nonsensical. They hadn't found their coin either, and Chadwick was blaming it all on the stupidity of his partner, who had gotten his wraps tangled up in a thorn bush.

Jason felt a surge of anger when he saw Fern, sitting under a tree laughing and animatedly telling Boris about her adventure. Boris had snakebites all over his arms and legs from Gorgonia, who was complaining to Bonestraggler about him.

At the sight of Fern, Jason began shaking with anger. He ran over to her. "Why did you lie?" he yelled.

Boris stood and blocked Jason from Fern. "Beat it, nerd!" he said, pushing Jason back.

Fern stood behind Boris, her hand to her mouth, giggling.

"There's no such thing as a Blue Pixie! I almost died!" Jason hollered.

"I don't know what you're talking about," said Fern. "You're the one who broke the chain because you wanted to find some weird pixie," she smirked.

"Liar!" shouted Jason.

"I already told everyone the story. You're in trouble," Fern remarked smugly.

"I said BEAT IT!" Boris shoved Jason again, this time sending him backwards.

From across the way, Argophemus saw what was happening and ran over.

"Hey," he shouted to Boris, "this is my roommate, and if I see you touch him one more time, I'll crush you with my bare hands." Argophemus stood a good two feet taller than Boris. His large eye was squinted and his forehead furrowed. Wisely, Boris backed down. He looked at his feet and mumbled something before turning away.

"And maybe YOU should start paying ME protection money for the summer!" Argophemus added.

"Thanks, Argophemus," Jason said, getting up from the ground.

He was stunned—all this time he'd thought Argophemus hated him.

"Yeah, yeah, yeah," Argophemus said, shrugging. "Don't tell anyone about this!" He scowled and walked away.

In the end, Bonestraggler was very angry not just because Jason and Fern had come back unattached, but also because they hadn't found their coin. He made Fern add more rocks to her lie-pile and assured them both that they would get a mark in Von Ulf's Red Book.

Chapter Eight

The Month of Full Moons

Jason sat in the office of his counselor, a slow-moving witch named Miss Harklestorm. She was very old with a narrow and wrinkly face, a long nose, and stringy gray hair. She always dressed in black robes and had an old frog named Butch that slept on her desk. Her office was cluttered with bottles of smoking and bubbling potions and books about spells, enchantments, and child psychology. She was an odd woman—constantly trying to invent anti-aging formulas and potions to give her clear, younger-looking skin, although none of them ever seemed to work. The last time she tested a potion to fix her wrinkles, she ended up with a corncob growing out of her ear.

Jason dreaded his Thursday afternoon appointments with Miss Harklestorm because she was usually in a terrible mood. The witch was obsessed with getting old and always accused Jason of thinking she was older than she actually was. The truth was, Jason thought she looked about 150 years old, but he would never tell her that.

Miss Harklestorm motioned for him to take a seat next to a bubbling cauldron.

"I'm just finishing a new potion," she said in a raspy voice, pointing to the large pot. "If all goes well, I'll have these wrinkles cleared up by the end of the day."

"Um...that's good news," said Jason.

"Just wait until you get old," she said sourly. "It's no picnic."

"Um...no, I'd imagine it isn't," agreed Jason, shifting

uncomfortably in his chair.

Miss Harklestorm took a seat behind her desk and slowly pulled out Jason's file with her long bony fingers. She sighed dramatically. "So, tell me about what happened in the woods this week. I hear you were written up again in the Red Book because of your fantastic imagination."

"It wasn't my fault," Jason started to explain. "Fern Pratt pushed me down the well, and I was almost attacked by a bunch of gremlins. I almost died!"

"Gremlins don't live in wells. They're afraid of water," the witch snapped. "You're supposed to be making progress here at the retreat, not going backwards."

"I just don't understand why I see things that other people can't," remarked Jason. "I'm not crazy," he added quietly.

"That's to be determined," the witch said.

At the same time, a loud beeping noise came out of the cauldron. It was the same strange sound Jason had been hearing since he arrived.

"Do you hear that?" he asked.

"Hear what?" Miss Harklestorm snapped impatiently.

"That beep! I hear it all the time," he said.

"I have no time for your poppycock," said the witch.

"It's not poppycock! I hear it!" said Jason.

"Are you insinuating that I am too old to hear things properly?" the witch asked, narrowing her eyes and glaring at Jason.

"No...forget it," Jason sighed.

"Tell me what you've learned here at the retreat," Miss Harklestorm commanded.

"Um...well...I've learned that monsters exist," said Jason,

saying the first thing that came to his mind.

"Don't be so generic!" snapped the witch. "What have you learned about living with the other inhabitants? What kinds of lessons have you learned?"

"Well...I've learned that everyone has a different idea about reality," he said. "I've learned that it's important to respect the ideas of others."

"What about *your* idea of reality?" asked the witch. "It's only gotten you in trouble so far. Don't you think you should try to adjust it?"

Jason thought for a moment. "I guess it's okay," he said. "I think I'd rather have an overactive imagination than none at all. Life would be pretty boring without it. It's weird...at home I used to dream about all these kinds of things—goblins, fairies, werewolves, and such—and it would get me into trouble. Now it's all really happening! No one will believe me when I get home, and no one believes me here. I can't win!"

The witch murmured something that sounded like, "*If* you go home."

"What did you say?" Jason asked.

"I said...um...er...answer the phone!" said Miss Harklestorm, pointing to a flowerpot.

"The phone isn't ringing," said Jason.

"Are you calling me senile?" asked the witch.

"No, ma'am."

"How old do you think I am, anyway?" she yelled.

Jason shrugged.

"Mr. Von Ulf has ways of teaching lessons," the witch said, changing the subject. "It's the first of August. I have a feeling things are going to start changing around here very soon." She

slowly hoisted herself up and hobbled over to the cauldron, dipped her finger in the bubbling potion, and tasted it. Her wrinkled face immediately turned a dark shade of purple. and a stem sprouted from the top of her head.

"What do you mean, things are going to start changing?" Jason asked, trying not to think of talking raisins.

"Just behave, and you'll be all right," she said, picking up a hand mirror. Then, upon seeing her "new look", she screamed so loud it shattered the glass.

That evening after dinner, Miles, Jason, and Chadwick sat on Jason's bunk playing cards. Ever since Dean had proven his existence to Chadwick late one night, the boy had been terrified of being alone. Just for a laugh, Dean had pretended he was going to bite Chadwick as he was sleeping. When Chadwick woke up and saw the vampire, Dean politely asked him not to use his bed as a desk anymore. Chadwick had been so frightened that he turned white as a ghost, dove under his covers, and didn't come out for two days. Three dwarfs had to come to the cabin, forcefully remove him from bed, and throw him in a cold shower to shock him back to reality. Chadwick hadn't been the same since. Now he mostly just sat and stared blankly ahead with a smelly ring of garlic around his neck, jumping at the slightest noise.

"I wonder what Miss Harklestorm meant when she said that soon things are going to change around here," Jason pondered, as he dealt the cards.

"Hopefully she meant Boris will be changed into a donkey!" Argophemus commented from across the room.

"I dunno" said Miles. "She seems to know a lot. She reads things from her crystal ball for me sometimes. According to her, I'm going to be a professional baseball player someday."

Argophemus snorted loudly and flipped the page of a music magazine he was reading. At that moment they heard a series of shrill screams coming from outside. The boys dropped their cards and huddled around the window. There, in the light of the full moon not too far from their cabin, Thelma Butterworth was standing in the middle of a large puddle of thick black mud with her arms crossed over her chest. There was a large gray wolf standing on its hind legs, slowly circling her and growling.

"Is that a...a...a...w-w-werewolf?" gasped Chadwick.

"Where?" Argophemus leaped down from his bed and climbed up next to the rest of them, shoving Chadwick out of the way and sending him toppling off of the bunk. He landed with a thud on the ground, bumping into Dean's coffin and causing it to rattle.

They watched as Thelma tried to lift her feet out of the mud. It was obvious that she was stuck.

Jason was both frightened and in awe of the werewolf. He had never seen a real live one before. The beast was large, at least seven feet tall. It was baring its fangs and frothing at the mouth. As it stood on its haunches, it swiped its long claws in the air towards Thelma.

"Shoo!" "Shoo!" yelled Thelma, waving her arms at the werewolf, all the while struggling to move her feet. All summer long she had been lazy, ignoring the leaders' orders to "get up, put that cupcake down, and keep moving!" Now there she was—stuck—and try as she might, she couldn't move.

Despite Thelma's cries, the werewolf didn't budge. Instead he lowered himself to the ground in a menacing stance, licked his lips, and watched her with his black eyes.

Thelma cried for someone to help, but nobody dared go near. Jason could see that the windows of all the surrounding cabins were filled with children, helplessly watching just as he and his roommates were. There was nothing that could be done. At one point, one of the dwarfs walked past carrying a bucket of carrots to the new centaur stable, but he didn't pay any attention to Thelma's cries for help.

"Well, as long as you don't come near me, I'll stand here all night. I don't care!" Thelma yelled, her voice shaking.

"What's she doing out there?" asked Jason.

"Maybe somebody should tell Von Ulf," said Miles.

"Are you joking?" laughed Argophemus, moving away from the window and jumping off the bed. He almost landed on Chadwick, who was leaning against the wall with his knees pulled to his chest, rocking back and forth.

"Why would I be joking?" Miles asked.

"Because that werewolf is Von Ulf," said Argophemus. "Look at the scar above his left eye."

Jason looked and sure enough, there was a white scar above the werewolf's eye—exactly where Von Ulf had one.

"But I thought werewolves were dangerous!" Miles cried. "How can he be in charge of us if he's a werewolf?"

"My father has known him for years," Argophemus explained. "Von Ulf used to be 100 percent human. He stumbled upon Fog Valley years ago and was bit by a werewolf in the woods. As a human he's pretty normal, but as a werewolf, well, he's unpredictable. He'll stay there all night until the sun comes up, and that's when he'll turn back into a human."

Jason and Miles exchanged wide-eyed glances.

"What's going to happen to Thelma?" Miles asked.

"I guess only time will tell," replied Argophemus, flopping back down on his own bed and pulling on his headphones.

Thelma was still stuck in the mud by the time the boys turned out the lights for the night. Jason tried to drown out her cries for help by putting his pillow over his head, but he could still hear her. He actually felt bad for Thelma. He was sure that Von Ulf was only teaching her a lesson and that she'd be all right, but it was still awful to think about her being stuck in the mud with a werewolf on the prowl. He sure wouldn't want to be in her shoes.

After a long night of restless sleep, Jason woke up to the sound of Thelma's screams, which sounded even more desperate now. He had a nervous feeling in his stomach as he looked out the window. Jason saw that the sun was shining, and the sky was blue. The werewolf was gone, but Thelma was *still* stuck in the black mud and had since sunken down to her waist! Now strange, twisting vines were sprouting up from the slop and wrapping around her like snakes. He could see Thelma pulling and tugging on the weeds with all of her might, trying to break free. Not more than 20 feet away, three dwarfs were busy working in the garden, completely aware of Thelma, but unconcerned about her dilemma.

"Why is no one helping her?" Jason gasped, loud enough to wake the others.

"What's going on?" asked Miles groggily.

"We have to help her!" Jason cried. He jumped down from his bunk and ran to the door. He turned the knob, but found that it was locked from the outside. His heart dropped. "We're locked in!"

"What?" Miles asked, his eyes wide. "Why?"

Argophemus jumped out of his bed and ran over to the door. He started pounding on it with his large fists, but the door wouldn't budge.

"Somebody has to help her!" Jason cried, climbing back up to the window. The others followed.

The vines had a tight grip on Thelma, and it was only getting tighter. She was beginning to sink down lower and lower into the mud.

"What's happening to her?" Jason cried. "What's pulling her down like that?"

"It's the seaweed people," Miles explained. "They live in the mud. When I was chained to Elgor on Outdoor Day, he told me all about them."

"Can't we do something?" Jason asked.

"She's doomed," said Argophemus, shaking his head. "Once they pull her into the mud, she will live with the seaweed people forever."

They all watched helplessly and in horror as Thelma Butterworth sank under the mud. The last thing they saw was the top of her head, a few bubbles, and then nothing.

Afterwards the boys remained huddled at the window. They were all in shock and disbelief about what they'd just seen. Then they heard a key turning in the lock and a letter was slipped under the door. Miles jumped down from the bunk, retrieved the letter, and began to read it aloud.

Dear Retreaters:

It is August in Fog Valley, *the Month of Full Moons.* Now comes the time to put all that you've learned at *Von Ulf's Retreat* to the test.

<u>Lesson for the day:</u>

Laziness is a disease that bogs one down in life. It sinks a person's soul deep into sorrow. Stubbornness is a personality trait that grabs hold of people who possess it and chokes the spirit. Don't let laziness and stubbornness weigh you down. Practice being active in life, setting goals, and being flexible. Otherwise you might find yourself tied in a knot that you can't escape from.

Sincerely,
Isaac Von Ulf

Jason couldn't believe what was happening. Thelma was gone. Sure, she wasn't anyone's favorite person—she was lazy and stubborn and didn't listen—but she didn't deserve this!

"It just doesn't make sense," Jason said. "How can Von Ulf get away with this? What will he tell Mr. and Mrs. Butterworth?"

"Who is Isaac Von Ulf anyway? I mean...*who is he?*" Miles said

"He's a legend here in Fog Valley," said Argophemus. "All the adults love him, and all of the children fear him."

"My parents just got a silly letter in the mail—that's how they found out about this camp," Miles said.

"Mine, too," said Chadwick.

"Yeah," said Jason, remembering the letter that Agnes had thrust at him in the car weeks earlier, "same with me." Then he remembered something else—something strange he had noticed about the letter. It was almost as if....

"If only I still had it," Jason said aloud.

"Still had what?" asked Miles.

"Wait!" Jason cried. It had suddenly dawned on him that the

letter should still be in the pocket of his jeans. "I think I do still have it!"

Jason dug through his bag and found the jeans. In the front pocket he found the letter that Agnes had received and brought it closer to his face. The ink was a bit faded from being in the wash a few times, but it was still legible.

"Chadwick, let me borrow your magnifying glass," said Jason. "It looks like it says something here."

Chadwick handed him the magnifying glass, and Jason held it up to the line of ink at the very bottom of the page. In tiny letters were these words:

*** Humans—there is no guarantee that your child will return at the end of three months. This will happen only if our behavioral goals are met.

Isaac Von Ulf will not be held responsible for unreturned children.

"It's not just Thelma," Jason said, lowering the magnifying glass with trembling hands. "We're *all* doomed."

Chapter Nine

A Perfect Plan

During the next weeks, a new tradgedy took place each day. Yolanda Jones had an unexpected encounter with a fire-spitting dragon. The beast scooped her up and flew away into the valley. Robby Bowman's candy days were over when a vegetarian giant chased him into the woods, where Robby would live with the giants forever. And Chadwick Wellington XVII was dragged through the mud and into the valley one night by an angry mob of centaurs, never to return. All of these catastrophes occurred during a full moon—right after a gray werewolf had chased the victim.

Fern Pratt met her fate as well. After sneaking out of her cabin one night to look for fairies, the werewolf chased her straight up the very pile of rocks she'd been amassing all summer long. She was stranded there until the early morning hours, when a group of winged harpies with the faces of angry women descended from the eastern sky. Using their long sharp talons, the harpies plucked Fern from her rockpile and carried her away into the clouds.

The following day the retreaters received another letter from Von Ulf.

> Dear Retreaters:
> Lesson for the day:
>
> Lying is a horrible habit. You may find that lies will build up to the point where one can't escape from them. Practice honesty, or you may one day become a prisoner of your own mounting lies.
>
> Sincerely,
> Isaac Von Ulf

After Boris had met his match—a family of angry ogres who pushed him around and sent him running for the hills, scared silly—Jason knew that his own time was running out. He knew now that Von Ulf's Retreat was not a place of reform, but a wicked institution existing only to destroy human children. He knew that if he didn't think of a way to escape, that he would be next. Late one night, Jason and his remaining roommates had an emergency meeting in their cabin.

"Miles and I have to find a way out of here somehow," whispered Jason. "Von Ulf is picking the humans off one by one, and I'm sure I'm next!"

"I could be next also," said Miles. "I'm sure the fact that I stood up to Bonestraggler the other day doesn't help matters."

"You did?" Jason asked, surprised.

"I was just so sick of him pinching me!" Miles said.

"Good for you!" Jason said. Throughout the summer Jason had noticed that Miles had changed. He was no longer the shy and fearful boy he'd met on the bus in the beginning of June; living among the monsters had made him more courageous. He had even stood up to Boris in those last days, refusing to give him protection money, which did result in his head being stuffed down the toilet and a few rounds of flushing, but it was worth it. Jason was proud of his friend.

"Well, even though we're not in any danger, Argophemus and I will do anything we can to help the two of you, won't we Argophemus?" Dean said.

"Sure," Argophemus shrugged, trying not to act like he cared. Jason had seen a change in Argophemus, too. He was a lot friendlier than he had been at first. Jason even thought he noticed a tear in Argophemus's big eye when he was told about Chadwick and the centaurs, but he denied it and insisted that it was just a piece of lint.

"You'll never be able to open that gate unless we can reach that lever, and we can't—it's impossible," Argophemus said. "Once it's shut, nobody leaves until the summer is over."

Argophemus was right. Jason remembered how the heavy gate had closed over the tunnel that first day of June, and the feeling he had of being locked in for the entire summer.

"What about that remote that the dwarfs used on the gate?" Jason asked. "Is there a way to get it?"

Argophemus shook his head. "The dwarfs guard that remote with their lives."

"If only we knew a giant, someone really tall who could pull the lever," said Miles.

"Right, because giants are really sweet and want to help humans. Just ask Robby Bowman," said Jason, sighing.

"And that's even if we can get you across the lake," Argophemus said. "The Kraken can eat you in a second."

"Hmmm…how to get across the lake?" Miles said, tapping his fingers on the bedpost.

They all sat deep in thought.

"I don't think there's a way…" Jason began, but then he suddenly remembered something. "Unless…."

"Unless what?" asked Dean.

Jason was thinking about the second week at the retreat, about the day they had the underwater challenge. He remembered that the mermaid Greta had rescued him from the weeds just before the Kraken got him. She had told him that she loved humans.

"Greta," Jason said. "Do you remember, I told you about her?"

"The mermaid?" Miles asked.

"Maybe she could get us across the lake!" Jason said

"Yes! That's a great idea!" said Miles excitedly. "I met Greta, too! She told me to whistle for her if I was ever in the area!"

"Really?" Jason said. "That's perfect!"

"There's still that lever." Argophemus sighed, pushing his long hair from his eye.

They sat in more silence, frustrated with their seemingly hopeless situation. Then suddenly Dean spoke up.

"There might be something I can do," he said quietly.

"What?" the others asked in unison.

"Well, I am a vampire," he said, nuzzling Miss Pinkerton's ears, "in case you forgot."

"So...what good does that do us?" Jason asked.

"On full moon nights, vampires can turn into bats if they feel like it," Dean said.

Jason immediately knew what Dean was thinking. Only someone who could reach the lever located above the jagged rocks could open the gate to freedom—only someone who could fly.

"You'd do that for us?" Jason asked excitedly.

"I would," said Dean. "Even though I think that becoming a bat is an old-fashioned ritual that demeans and objectifies vampires, I'd do it for you."

"Thanks, Dean!" said Jason.

"Yes, thank you, Dean!" Miles added, smiling.

Dean sat up straight and puffed out his chest. "Call me Vlad," he said.

⁓⁓⁓⁓⁓⁓⁓⁓⁓⁓⁓⁓⁓⁓⁓⁓⁓⁓⁓⁓⁓⁓⁓⁓⁓⁓⁓⁓⁓⁓⁓⁓⁓⁓⁓⁓

By morning the plan was in place. Later that day, while Miles was working in the garden, he made an excuse to go to the lake to collect some reeds. He whistled for Greta, who was very happy to see him. The mermaid agreed that later that night she would meet them at the shore and guide Jason and Miles safely over the lake. Once across, Vlad—in the form of a bat—would be waiting near the gate in the woods. When he saw them approaching, he would pull the lever to open the gate to the tunnel, where the train of carts would be waiting. Jason and Miles would then ride back home, away from Fog Valley and Von Ulf's horrible retreat forever. It seemed like a flawless plan.

The day was a trying one for Jason. Von Ulf seemed to know that he was up to something. The headmaster watched Jason as he worked in the kitchen all day, waiting for the chance to write him up. He also stared at Jason during dinner, licking his lips and anxiously looking out the window, as if he couldn't wait for the sun to go down.

After dinner Jason and Miles nervously sat in their cabin waiting for nightfall. A steady rain began to fall, and low thunder rumbled and echoed through the valley. When the sun went down, the now familiar sounds of howling werewolves mixed with the sounds of the storm.

"What's taking Dean so long?" asked Miles, nervously looking at the coffin. "Shouldn't he be awake by now?"

"He's a late sleeper," explained Jason. "It's one of the things that made his father so angry with him."

"Well, I can't wait anymore!" Miles jumped up and began pacing around the room. "I keep expecting a werewolf to come crashing through the window and chase us off of a cliff or something."

"He'll be awake soon," said Jason. "Dean would never let us down."

Sure enough, at around half past midnight, the vampire emerged from his coffin. He yawned, dusted himself off, then went to the bathroom to brush his fangs and comb his hair.

"Ready?" he asked, emerging from the bathroom.

"Ready as we'll ever be," said Miles, wringing his fingers and bouncing nervously.

"We can't thank you enough, Dean...I mean...Vlad. You're saving our lives," said Jason.

"No problem," said Vlad. "You know, I'll really miss you guys."

"We'll miss you, too," Jason said. "Good luck with everything... especially your father. Don't ever change."

Vlad smiled and winked. "Just this once," he said. Then there was a loud POP! followed by a plume of white smoke.

Jason gasped. A small black bat with red eyes and leathery, black wings fluttered where Vlad had stood. The bat let out a piercing scream, circled the room once, and then flew into the stormy night, followed by Miss Pinkerton.

The scream woke Argophemus briefly. He said goodbye to his roommates, wished them well, and then went back to sleep.

"Ready?" asked Jason.

"I'm ready," Miles nodded.

They quietly opened the door and stepped out into the rainy night. The storm seemed to be getting worse. Thunder echoed from the walls of the mountain and electric flashes of lightning lit up the valley below. The late summer wind blew fiercely, howling almost as loudly as the werewolves in the distance. Slowly Jason and Miles made their way down the muddy mountain path, ducking behind trees so they wouldn't be seen and trying to avoid puddles for fear of sinking into an unexpected abyss as Thelma had.

It was while they were crouched behind a tree that Jason heard the cracking of twigs and rustling of leaves, and then a cold hand tightly gripped on to his shoulder. Alarmed, he jumped up and spun around. He was now looking straight into the dead, black-rimmed eyes of a vampire. Jason's own eyes widened in horror, and suddenly he felt very dizzy.

"Oh, no," said Miles.

Standing before them were three tall and thin vampires. They had pale faces and gaunt cheeks, and looked as if life itself had been drained from them. They stood staring at the boys. Jason could tell that the vampires were nothing like Dean—they were the real deal, and they were looking for blood. Miles and Jason stood against a nearby tree, frozen in fear.

"Vhat do ve have here?" asked one of the vampires in a low voice as he licked his pale lips.

"It appears vhat some human children have come to dinner," said the vampire standing in the center of the group.

"Please, w-w-we don't want any trouble," Jason stuttered nervously. "W-w-we were just leaving."

"Leaving so soon?" the tallest one asked. "But you've only just arrived."

"No, we've been here long enough," said Jason. "It's time we left."

One of the vampires threw his head back and let out a sinister, hollow laugh. "Don't you vant to be immortal?" he asked. "Live forever?"

"Not if it means being a vampire!" exclaimed Jason.

Suddenly one of the vampires lurched forward and grabbed Miles, and the one who had gripped Jason's shoulder now grabbed it again, tightening his hold and drawing Jason closer. The boys

both kicked and screamed, struggling to break free, but it was no use.

"Ve do love the taste of human blood," cackled the third vampire, the tallest one of them all.

The vampire holding Miles opened his mouth wide, baring two sharp fangs, and slowly lowered his teeth towards Miles's neck.

"NO! WAIT!" Jason cried.

The vampire came within an inch of biting Miles and then stopped.

"You're time has run out," said the tall vampire. "It's time that you join us."

"No, please! Not yet!" Jason yelled.

"Vhy don't you vant to live forever?" said the vampire who was holding him.

"Well, for one thing...our roommate Dean...I mean Vlad...tells us it's a very lonely life," Jason said, stalling for time.

At the mention of Vlad, the tallest vampire's eyes widened in surprise. "Did you say Vlad?"

"Y-yes," stuttered Jason. "He's our roommate at Von Ulf's Retreat For Unruly Youths."

"Vlad is my son," said the vampire. "Tell me, how is he doing?"

"He's fine," said Jason. "He's one of my best friends at the retreat. He misses you and wishes that you could accept him for the way he is."

"Vlad is my biggest disappointment," said the vampire, shaking his head. Jason couldn't be sure, but he thought he saw a hint of pride come over his pale face. "But he is a good boy. He means vell, I guess. I know he'd be very upset if I hurt his friends." Then to Jason's surprise, the vampire motioned to the others to let them free.

"Run along. Don't let us catch you here again," Vlad's father. said, in spite of the other two vampires' protests.

"No, sir, you won't!" cried Jason, and with that, he and Miles continued sprinting down the path towards the lake, this time not bothering to hide behind trees.

When they reached the lake, Greta was in the water waiting for them with a large smile on her face. She had long blond hair and blue eyes, and from the waist up she looked like a normal girl. But when she dove into the water, her scaly green tail fin confirmed that she wasn't human.

Greta clapped her hands when she saw the boys. "I'm so happy to be able to help you! Both of you, grab onto my tail and hold your breath!" she said, smiling. "I'll get you two across just fine!"

They each grabbed hold of Greta's scaly tail and held on as she plunged underwater.

The water was cold. Jason couldn't help but open his eyes and watch as Greta took them past ornate sandcastle houses, strange fish of every color and shape, and bubbling underwater volcanoes. She stopped every few moments to surface and give them air. At one point Jason could see the eye of the Kraken and its long black tentacles coming towards them, but Greta was too fast for it—she had them across the lake in no time at all.

"Thanks so much, Greta!" Miles said, as he scrambled to the shore.

"No problem, friends!" Greta cried. "I hope you come back to visit me some day!"

"Sure we will!" said Jason, crossing his fingers behind his back.

Greta waved once more before diving back underwater, leaving the two of them alone on the shore, dripping wet and minutes away from escape. However, they weren't alone.

As the boys turned to make their way through the woods to the gate, they both stopped dead in their tracks. Jason felt his heart sink. A few yards ahead of them stood Isaac Von Ulf.

"Going somewhere?" Von Ulf asked, leaning on his walking stick and staring straight into Jason's eyes.

"Yes. We're getting out of here," Jason said confidently, "and you can't stop us!"

"But you only have one week left!" Von Ulf said. "You know I can't return you home before you are 100 percent reformed. And you two haven't improved, as far as I can see."

"We never should have been sent here in the first place!" yelled Miles.

"Obviously the two of you are in denial and have a long way to go before you're ready to return home," said Von Ulf.

"I read the fine print on your letter. You're not interested in reforming us, you only want to kill us!" Jason yelled.

"I don't know what you mean by trying to escape. I'm not trying to kill you or anyone," Von Ulf said, slowly moving closer.

"Oh, yeah? What about Chadwick? What about Thelma Butterworth and little Robby Bowman? What about Boris Stubbs? You had him baked into a pie for ogres to eat!" Jason said.

"Such a fantastic imagination," Von Ulf chortled, shaking his head.

"I'm not imagining it. You did it!" Jason shouted. "All to try and prove some stupid lesson!"

"Those children met their consequence because they didn't learn to correct their weaknesses," Von Ulf explained, matter-of-factly. "You'd better be careful. The same thing might happen to you if you don't take control of that imagination of yours. It might get you into a lot of trouble."

"Or maybe it will save me!" Jason said. A flash of lightning lit up the valley, followed by a crash of thunder. In the distance, coming from the direction of the gate, he heard the beeping sound again.

"You know, I can't let you leave," Von Ulf said calmly.

At that moment Jason knew what was going to happen next. He felt the same way all of the others must have felt before Von Ulf had taught them their "lesson of the day." Jason watched in horror as Von Ulf's face slowly began to melt. His features became blurred and right before their eyes, he morphed into something grotesque. His body suddenly took on the form of a gray wolf. Long whiskers sprouted from his cheeks, and his nose took the shape of a snout. His teeth grew long over his lower lip, turning into sharp fangs that were three times their regular size. Soon he stood on his haunches, drooling and growling, and began circling the boys like a shark.

"Now what do we do?" whispered Miles.

"On the count of three, we split up and run," said Jason. "Meet me at the gate. One...two...THREE!"

The two boys took off running in different directions. The werewolf immediately followed Jason, who got a good 10 yards ahead, but Von Ulf quickly gained on him. Jason ran as fast as he could through the woods towards the gate. Branches cracked underneath his feet as the rain continued to fall. He could hear his heart pounding through his chest and the steady trot of Von Ulf's paws behind him. Just then he felt a piercing pain shoot through his right leg, and he fell. Von Ulf had bitten him and was now coming back for more.

Jason kicked with both legs as hard as he could, sending the werewolf backwards for a moment. Then he pulled himself back up from the ground and ran. Jason looked down at his leg and saw the two fang marks where Von Ulf had nipped him. Luckily the wet ground had caused the werewolf to slide and crash into a fallen tree limb. This gave Jason some more time to get ahead.

Jason continued to run. The blood from the fang marks dripped down to his shoes and the wound stung, but still he ran, ignoring the sound of growling and barking that now was just seconds behind him. Was this how the other children felt as Von Ulf the werewolf chased them? What did Von Ulf have in store for him? What was the punishment for having an overactive imagination?

Just then, Jason spotted the tunnel. He looked up and caught a glimpse of a bat circling around the rocky ledge high above the gate. On the ledge, peering over the side and wriggling her nose, was Miss Pinkerton.

"Dean!" Jason cried. "Now! Do it now!"

When he saw Jason, the bat flapped its wings, pushing the lever. The gate began to open. Jason was almost there.

"I want to live!" Jason screamed. "I want to go home!"

As Jason was seconds away from the tunnel, a huge gust of wind blew. It seemed to Jason as if everything was moving in slow motion. He looked up. From the corner of his eye, he watched in horror as Miss Pinkerton was swept up by the strong wind. At that moment the bat let out a horrified screech, and in an instant, he morphed back into Dean.

"Noooooo!" Dean cried, standing on the ledge looking down. "Miss Pinkerton!" The chubby vampire watched helplessly as the

wind sent his beloved pet plummeting into the tunnel.

Jason's last sights of Fog Valley were the open jaws of the werewolf behind him, and his friend's heartbroken face above. The sound of the beep got louder and louder, and the lightning in the sky was brighter than ever. Jason knew what he had to do. He dove into the tunnel and simultaneously saw an electric FLASH! He felt himself falling and then everything went black.

Chapter Ten

The Return

Jason woke up in a hospital bed, soaking wet with sweat. His wrist was wrapped in a bandage and his head ached.

Staring down at him was a doctor, a nurse, and Agnes. Next to him, Oliver lay in a bed surrounded by flowers and balloons with his leg wrapped in a full cast. He was sitting upright eating ice cream. A small puppy was in his lap, and Mrs. Jensen was perched above him like a watchful bird, smoothing his hair and cooing words of endearment.

"He's awake!" cried out the doctor.

"It's a miracle!" said the nurse who wore a nametag that said Wilhelmina.

The doctor leaned down and shone a bright light into Jason's eyes. FLASH!

"Look to the left," he said.

Jason did.

"Look to the right," he said.

Jason did.

"Do you know where you are?" asked the doctor.

"I...I'm at Von Ulf's Retreat." Jason murmured.

There was a steady beep coming from the heart rate monitor next to Jason's bed.

He was very confused.

"Still talking nonsense, hmm?" said the doctor.

"He's always had a very active imagination," Agnes pointed out.

"Bumps on the head can make you say odd things," remarked the nurse.

"You're a lucky kid!" said the doctor. "You've been unconscious for four days!"

"Four...what?" said Jason. He felt groggy and very confused.

"That's right," said the nurse, "four days. We were very concerned about you. You had a very serious head injury."

"For a while we thought we had lost you," said the doctor. "It really is a miracle. At one point you were literally slipping away...it was as if someone just came and pulled you up from danger!"

Suddenly everything became clear. Jason remembered that he and Oliver had been on top of Hickory Hill. They had built a cart and called it...called it.

"I Von Ulf," Jason said aloud. "I Lov Fun..."

"I love fun," the doctor chuckled, "that's some imagination you have. You should've heard some of the things you were mumbling while you were unconscious: fairy wings, Faun Stew, looking for coins in the forest! Lucky for you that you have such a grand imagination," the doctor added. "You know, studies show that the more active the imagination, the more likely one is to survive a head injury like this one. You just made it!"

So Jason had almost died, but his imagination quite literally had saved him. He looked down at his leg. There were two puncture wounds, located in the exact same place that Von Ulf had bitten him.

"What's that?" said Jason, remembering clearly the pain he had felt when the wolf had bit him.

"When you crashed into the hair salon, you collided with a pair of scissors," explained the doctor.

"Oh, thank goodness you are all right!" cried Agnes. While no one was looking, Jason saw her take out a bottle of eye drops and squirt them into her eyes to create phony tears.

A week later Jason was ready to go home. His father, who had returned from his trip after hearing about Jason's accident, surprised his son by coming to check him out of his hospital room: room #13. On the way to the car, his father talked about how lucky Jason was to have survived.

"I just don't know what I would have done if I lost you, son," said his father, ruffling his hair. "You must have a guardian angel somewhere."

"I think I do," said Jason, smiling to himself.

"Agnes is going to be so happy to have you home," said his father. "She's been worried sick about you!"

Jason grinned and shook his head. *Agnes.* Somehow after his ordeal, Agnes didn't seem like such a monster anymore.

They reached the car, and Jason opened the passenger side door. On the front seat was a package in red wrapping with a big silver ribbon tied around it.

"What's this?" asked Jason.

"It's a welcome home gift," said his father. "Better open it quickly," he added.

Jason tore off the red paper to reveal a cardboard box with several holes poked into it. He carefully opened the box and looked inside.

"I thought you could use a pet," said his father with a huge grin on his face.

Jason gasped when he saw what was in the box. There, curled up

on a fluffy blanket, was a little brown ferret with long whiskers and a white stripe down its back. It lifted its head and winked at Jason.

He knew exactly what he'd name it.